CLEAN SLATE

THE GOODE LIFE #1

ISLA OLSEN

Copyright 2021 Isla Olsen

All rights reserved. No part of this book may be reproduced, distributed or transmitted in any form or by any means without the express written permission of the author, except for the use of brief quotations in an article or book review.

All people, events and places featured in this book are products of the author's imagination or used in a fictitious context. Any resemblance to real persons, living or dead, is purely coincidental.

Cover Copyright 2021 Cate Ashwood

❦ Created with Vellum

ABOUT THE GOODE FAMILY

Nora and Ted Goode had four children, all boys. They are:

Bennett, who married Eloise and had two children of his own: Webster (Web) and Kip

Walker, who married Genevieve and had five children of his own: Axel, Slater, Tansie, Everley, and Tucker.

Carson, who never married Lorelai but nevertheless managed to upstage his brothers with a brood of six: Candace, Livia, Harriett, Delia, Poppy, and (finally, the boy Carson always wanted!) George.

…and Rock, a late in life baby who gives his mother no end of grief by insisting he'll remain a bachelor for eternity.

PROLOGUE

Zack

"That didn't happen," I gasp out the moment I manage to recover my breath. I stare determinedly at the ceiling of Slater Goode's bedroom, praying that if I put just enough conviction into the statement I can make it true. I'm also praying for the ability to disapparate like in *Harry Potter*, and for the formula for the flux capacitor so I can build a time machine out of my rental car. Anything that could get me out of this situation.

Of course, my prayers go unanswered, leaving me stuck in this bed with the one person I *so* should not have woken up with this morning. Along with all the dirty, dirty memories of last night—and five minutes ago—running through my brain on a never-ending loop.

Oh my God, what the fuck was I thinking? *Slater Goode?* I slept with *Slater Goode!* Several times!

I keep praying for that time machine, but I'm not really holding out much hope. I've never really been big on organized religion and I doubt the big guy's going to start doling out favors for me now. Not to mention...oh, that's right, time travel is impossible—it's called living with the consequences of your actions. *Damn you, Drunk Zack, why do you always ruin life for Sober Zack?*

I feel the bed shift under Slater's weight and then he's hovering over me, flashing that boner-inducing grin of his. "I'm pretty sure it did, babe. In fact, I'm pretty sure that was your idea."

I groan, lifting a hand to cover my face. Because, yes, I *may* have initiated that round, but I'm holding my cock responsible. That guy just doesn't know what's good for him.

In truth, the past twelve hours have included several rounds of the best sex of my life, but I can't admit that. Not to Slater. I don't care how amazing his smile is, or how sexy he looks with his golden hair all messed up like that. *From my hands yanking at it while he was pounding inside me just now...* Fuck, I need to get a grip.

I may have let my guard slip a little—okay, a lot—in recent hours, but I need to remember Slater Goode is still the guy who shattered my heart into a million pieces twelve years ago. My needy cock and thoroughly-sated body might be trying to convince me to let him off the hook, but my brain knows better.

"No no no...no! God! No!!" I shake my head in desperate denial.

"It's amazing," Slater says in his sexy gravelly voice, "you were screaming the exact opposite of that only a a few minutes ago." His chocolate brown eyes are dancing with mirth.

I squeeze my own eyes shut to avoid looking into them. Those eyes are my one major weakness. Well, unless you count the smile. And that incredible body. And...god damn it, why can't he be hideous? But those eyes...in spite of all my best efforts to reform, it seems one heated gaze from him is still all it takes to make my bones melt.

I open my own eyes again and dare to meet his gaze, my breath catching at the look of raw desire he has me pinned with. Taking advantage of my momentary lapse, he dips his head to take one of my nipples in his mouth. And oh, my lord...

I can't help letting out a soft groan at the contact as heat floods through me. My cock is making a valiant effort to get in on the action; it's like that drunk guy at the end of a party who won't go home until he has 'just one more.'

Fortunately, for my sanity, I'm physically incapable of getting further into this right now and so it doesn't take long for my brain to take back control. I give Slater a firm shove and he rolls off me and onto his back, his face stretched into a teasing grin.

If only I'd managed to have that kind of control over my senses last night... But that's the human body for you: your body says one thing, your brain says another (or in this case has its mouth duct-taped shut by a little prankster called tequila), and the next thing you know, you're in the bathroom at your ex-boyfriend's grandfather's wake and you've got his fingers inside your ass. The ex-boyfriend's. Not the grandfather's. 'Cause that would be gross. And I'm pretty sure illegal.

Okay, I need to get out of this bed. And get dressed. And leave.

I spring up off the mattress and begin to turn over the room searching for my clothes. I can feel Slater's eyes stalking me as I gather my scattered clothes and start to dress. I stare in dismay as I pick up my shirt and notice a bunch of the buttons have been torn off.

"Seriously, Slater?" I ask, sending a frustrated glare in his direction.

He merely shrugs, offering me a smirk. "You want to borrow one of mine?"

"No," I say with absolute conviction before threading my arms through the sleeves of the torn shirt. A one-time sex-only backslide is one thing; borrowing clothes is an entirely different situation.

I tuck my shirt into my pants and then grab my tie, figuring if I tie it just right it might hide the open shirt from anyone who looks too closely. Not that anyone who sees me in a suit the morning after the funeral won't make assumptions anyway…

"Look, Slater, last night—"

"And this morning," he cuts in.

I close my eyes, taking a deep breath. "And this morning. It was…fun."

"Oh I think we can both agree it was pretty mind-blowing." He chuckles. "Like riding a bike, hey babe?"

I press my fingers to my forehead. "The point is, it was a one-night only deal. Call it a bonus night or whatever. It's over now. We're done."

"If you say so."

I nearly jump out of my skin, because the voice came from right behind me. I was focusing on my tie and didn't hear Slater move from the bed, but now he's hovering right at my back, his breath heating my neck and causing a full-body shiver to run through me. He gently grips my waist and turns me to face him, then takes hold of each end of my tie.

I nod, feeling a little off-kilter as I stand there allowing him to fix my tie. "Yes. I do say so."

"Mmmhmm." He finishes the knot and smoothes the tie down.

"Why don't you believe me?"

"Because you're not being very convincing." He gives my tie a little tug, pulling me closer to him. And as his lips descend on mine, my brain once again fails to function; what's one more kiss in the grand scheme of things, right?

1

SIX DAYS EARLIER

From the private Facebook group 'Finchley Locals Community Hangout'

Post by Chance Kingsley: Reminder - the FHS baseball alumni cook-out starts at 12pm today at mine and Slater's place. We'll provide the food, you bring the drinks
Tansie Goode reply to Chance Kingsley's post: And by "you" you really only mean former Finchley High baseball players
Chance Kingsley reply to Tansie Goode's comment: That's kind of what baseball alumni means *wink emoji*
Tansie Goode reply to Chance Kingsley's comment: I call discrimination!

*Chance Kingsley reply to Tansie Goode's comment:
What can I say? You weren't on the baseball team in high school *shrug emoji**
Tansie Goode reply to Chance Kingsley's comment: They didn't allow girls on the baseball team in high school!
Chance Kingsley reply to Tansie Goode's comment: Now that's discrimination - take it up with FHS though, we're just grilling burgers here

Slater

I'm lying on the bank of Dewer Lake, one of my favorite little spots about a half hour's drive out of Finchley, the little town in California's Gold Country that I've called home my entire life. The sun's beating down on me with the heat of a perfect early fall afternoon, and I'm just starting to consider a dip in the water to cool off for a bit when Zac Efron appears next to me with a bottle of sunblock in hand.

He looks hot as fuck in a nothing but a pair of tight black swim shorts, and he just smiles at me as he squirts a whole heap of sunblock onto my chest and starts rubbing it in. I don't usually bother with sunblock, it's such a pain in the ass, but if Zac wants to watch out for my skin I am totally on board with that.

"Slate," he says with a smile.

I just stare at him with a big goofy grin on my face.

"Slater," he says again. Then his smile becomes a pout. "Slate, wake up."

Uh, no thanks.

He slaps me a few times on the cheek, and this time when he speaks it's in my cousin Webster's gruff voice, which is fucking creepy. "Wake the fuck up, dumbass!"

I finally snap out of my dream and become gradually aware of my real surroundings. It's daylight. Hot. I'm in my backyard, I think. There are empty beer bottles scattered all over the ground—well, that would explain why my head hurts so much.

"You're not Zac Efron," I grumble at Web who's hovering over me, my eyes blinking rapidly as I adjust to the waking world.

"Well spotted, dipshit."

There are other guys milling around the yard as well. I groan. Right—the barbeque. It was up to my roommate, Chance, and me to host this year's get together with all the old guys from Finchley High's baseball team and by the looks of things we pulled it off pretty well.

Now that I'm more fully awake I notice a weird tickling sensation on my torso. Looking down, I find a combination of what must be every condiment from my kitchen pantry has been drizzled and smeared over my bare chest and now flies have started in on me, eager for some lunch.

The fuckers. My own fault, I guess. It's common knowledge around here that if you pass out in a public place or group situation you should expect to wake up in a somewhat compromised state.

"Do I have a dick on my face?" I ask Web.

He snorts a laugh. "Not this time."

I pat my hands over my face. Thank fuck. My eyebrows are still there. I scrub my hand through my hair and it feels normal. I don't think I could have slept through a dye job, but it's been known to happen to others.

"Your hair's fine, too," Web assures me.

I glance around, studying the suspects carefully. Most of them are smiling or laughing; it's been a long time since I've been caught out like this. Chance and another of my cousins, George, however, are both studiously avoiding eye contact with me. Bingo. I should've known George would be behind this; he's about as mature as my four-year-old nephew. As for Chance, well his position as my roommate comes with easy access to the condiments currently forming a crust on my skin. Add to that the fact that neither one of those assholes can make eye contact with me right now and it's case closed.

I get up and head off into my shed to grab the sponges and buckets I use to clean my truck. It'd be quicker just to use the hose, but after growing up with years of intermittent drought, you learn not to waste water. Besides, this will be more fun.

After filling two buckets with lukewarm, sudsy water I carry them over to George and Chance and place one at each of their feet.

"Seeing as how you boys love running your hands all over my hot bod, how'd you like to wash me down?"

I hear a chorus of laughter behind me and sense the rest of the guys gathering around to watch the spectacle.

Chance and George look at each other for a moment, shrug, then get on with it.

I stretch my arms out and let them do their thing, which takes a surprisingly long time; some of the condiments they used have dried out in the sun and caked onto my skin, making it hard for the guys to clean off.

"Stop laughing, Slate!" Chance says, throwing me a frustrated look under the bill of his Lakers cap.

"I can't help it! George's got that look my mom gets when she's scrubbing the range."

"If by 'that look' you mean fucking sexy then I'll gladly accept the compliment," the bastard says with a grin. "I can just imagine it, Aunt Gen wearing some of those pink rubber gloves, maybe her shirt gets a little wet from the dishwater."

"Watch it, fucker," I snap, yanking the sponge away from him. My mom was only seventeen when she had my older brother, Axel, and she's still looking pretty good at forty-nine. Needless to say, Ax and I have been on the end of countless MILF jokes over the years. Although, I've got admit, I did open myself right up for that one.

"Dude, that's your aunt. What's wrong with you?" Chance says to George, as if there's an actual answer to that question.

George merely shrugs. "Only by marriage."

"That's enough. I can get the rest later," I tell them.

They've gotten most of the gunk off me, but there's still some encrusted in the hair on my lower abdomen. Just as well I'm not rocking the Wolverine look like some of the other guys or this could have ended in an impromptu amateur waxing job.

I've just finished toweling myself off when a three-and-a-half-foot blur of red and blue comes bolting around the side of the house to crash right into my legs.

"Uncle Slate! Uncle Slate! Grandpa Ted had an accident!"

I detach my four-year-old nephew, Ethan, from my legs and crouch down so I'm eye-level with him. He's dressed in the Spiderman costume I got him for his last birthday and is wearing an incredibly somber expression for such a little kid.

"E, what are you talking about? What happened to Grandpa?" With Ethan an 'accident' could be anything from cutting a finger to falling off a ladder, but the way he's looking at me right now definitely has me thinking it's something pretty serious.

"Him and Nanna were eating spicy food and the prostigate hurt his heart," Ethan says with a sniffle.

I blink at him a few times, trying to make sense of his words. What the hell's 'prostigate?' My mind races for some sort of food item that Ethan's four-year-old brain has replaced with that made up word but I'm drawing blanks. Then I land on the last part of what he told me. "Wait—his heart hurt? Like, he had a heart attack?"

I can tell by the look on my nephew's face he's not really sure what I'm asking, but I get my answer anyway. His lip quivers and then he throws himself into my arms. "His heart broked, Slater."

I hold my nephew tight, rubbing my hands over his back as I try to come to terms with the fact that, unless Ethan's completely misunderstood the situation, the man that has been like a second father to me died today. All around me, I sense people closing in. I glance up to see Web, George, and Axel all hovering around me. Each of them are wearing expressions of dread, their faces drained of color.

"Ethan! I told you to wait for me!" I hear my mother's voice, full of exasperation, as she rounds the corner of my house and appears in the backyard.

I let go of Ethan and stand up to approach her. "Is it true?"

"Mom, what's going on?" Axel presses.

Mom lets out a deep sigh, her eyes full of sadness as her gaze travels from me to Ax and then to our cousins and the other guys who have gathered around. "I'm sorry, boys."

"What happened? Was it really a heart attack?" It's Web who asks. He's standing right beside me now, his face drawn and pale.

Mom glances around the yard for a moment, obviously looking to see where Ethan is. He's sitting on the back steps with Chance, who's taken off his cap and is letting Ethan inspect it, no doubt attempting to convert him to the Lakers.

Seeing Ethan is well-occupied, Mom turns her attention back to us. She takes a deep breath before she starts talking. "It was an accident…" she hesitates for a moment, biting her lip. "Of the coital nature."

I blink at her a few times, my mouth parting in confusion. "Come again?"

"They were…" She waves a hand about in a circular

motion, as though searching for the right word. "Experimenting. It happens sometimes, you know. When you've been married a long time it's important to keep things fresh. Interesting.'

"Mom—stop!" I hold up a hand in dismay. "You're obviously mistaken. They couldn't have been having sex. They're grandparents."

"What does that have to do with anything?" Mom asks, brows raised in question. "Your father and I are grandparents and we still—"

I hold my hand out to halt her words, shaking my head furiously. "No, no. This day is horrible enough without hearing this!"

"Dude, of course they were still having sex—that's what Viagra's for," George says with a roll of his eyes. Then he turns to my mom. "What was this 'experiment', Aunt Gen?"

"George…" Web shakes his head at the question. "I really don't think that's necessary.'

George shrugs. "I think it's important to learn from this tragedy. I don't want to be having sex and worrying that it's going to kill me." He looks up wistfully, adding, "But what a way to go."

I cut George a sharp look. "Dude, that's our grandfather."

He has the decency to look somewhat sheepish, but I know he's still wondering exactly what happened, and I guess I can't blame him—with the amount of sex George has, it's got to be freaking him out to learn of someone actually dying in the act. But I, for one, don't need to know any more about my grandparents' exploits, so I'm glad when my mom ignores his question.

"How's Nanna?" I ask her.

Mom lets out a deep sigh. "She's doing okay, considering. Fifty-seven years…" she adds with a sad shake of her head.

"Interesting that that's how old your dad is, Web," George says with a teasing smirk.

"Can I punch him?" Web grunts.

Ignoring my cousins, I reach out and wrap my arms around Mom, pulling her against my chest. Nanna and Grandpa are my paternal grandparents, but they're the only parents my mom has known ever since her own kicked her out when she got pregnant with Ax, as if it were the 1880s and not the 1980s. I know this has to be hitting her hard.

"Do the girls know?" I ask. "And Tucker?"

Mom nods. "Everley's driving down to tell Tucker and bring him home." Well, that would explain why Mom's watching Ethan; I can't imagine my sister would want to bring him along for the drive to Davis. "And Tansie's with Lorelai's girls," she adds, resorting to the widely-used collective term for George's five older sisters. "They're working out the details for the funeral and things like that."

"Already?"

Mom offers a sad smile. "These things move quickly, honey. You know how this town is, and how important Ted was to it…" she trails off, letting out a soft sigh.

Was. The word hits me hard and sharp in the chest. I'm

not ready to hear my grandfather referred to in the past tense. I'm not ready for him to be gone at all.

AFTER SENDING all our high school buddies on their way, we leave Chance in charge of the clean up and Web, George, and I go to pay a visit to Nanna.

I pull up out the front of Nanna and Granddad's house —the house that has always been like a second home to me—and we all pile out of my truck. Out of a force of habit that for some reason I haven't been able to shake for the past twelve years, my gaze automatically drifts to the house to the right of my grandparents', where my high school boyfriend, Zack, used to live. But just as quickly, I look away, reminding myself—yet again—there's no point dwelling on the decisions I made back then, or how I would change it if I could. The truth is, half the time I'm sure I wouldn't change a damn thing.

Nanna doesn't come to the door straight away, so after a few minutes of waiting and intermittent knocking, I grab the spare key out of the potted plant by the door and let us inside. The house is dark and gloomy—the complete opposite of what I've come to expect upon entering my grandparents' house.

"What the fuck is that smell?" Web asks, his face screwed up in distaste.

"Holy shit—is that smoke?"

I follow George's wide-eyed gaze down the center hallway and out the back window to my grandparents' yard. Where a fire seems to be roaring in the bonfire pit out there.

"What the hell is she burning?" George's expression is uncharacteristically serious. "It smells like...plastic."

"C'mon." I head down the hallway and gesture for the boys to follow after me. When I get outside, I see my grandmother fervently stoking the fire, a determined look on her face. "Nanna?"

Her head snaps around at the sound of my voice, her eyes wide with alarm and...fear?

"Oh, boys—you shouldn't be here!"

My brows draw together in concern. "Of course we should. We came to see how you are."

She's in her late seventies, but until today, she didn't look it. It's scary to think how drastically she's aged overnight, but I guess that's just what happens when the person you've loved for over fifty years is ripped away from you so suddenly.

In a defeated gesture, Nanna tosses the poker aside before burying her face in her hands, her body heaving with desperate sobs. I rush to throw my arms around her, drawing her into my chest the same way I did for my mother just an hour ago. "I thought I would have more time," she says in a ragged wail. I'm assuming she's referring to time with my grandfather, but then she says, "I didn't realize you'd be here so quickly."

"Huh?" I lean my head back so I can look at her properly. "Nanna, what're you talking about?"

She looks up at me, her eyes wide with fear. "I thought I'd be able to destroy the evidence and no one would ever know..."

"No one would know what?"

She breaks out of my hold, her hands flying up in a

gesture of surrender. "That I killed him, Slater! With that...thing!" She points angrily at the bonfire before beginning to pace a short path back and forth, her hands clawing at her hair. "I can't go to prison! Do you know what they do to people like me in prison?"

I exchange a baffled glance with George and Web, and I can tell they're thinking the exact same thing I am: *No? what the hell do they do to old ladies with a passion for knitting and baking pie in prison?*

With a shake of my head, I turn to my grandmother, leveling her with a firm look. "Nanna—you didn't kill anyone. Grandpa died of a heart attack."

"Yes—because of me. Because of that thing!" She once again gestures wildly at the bonfire.

Sharing another curious glance with George and Web, we each step closer to the fire to see what all the fuss is about. The object in question seems to be made of silicone, and is clearly very flame retardant, because it doesn't take me long to figure out what it is. I let out a groan of dismay once I realize what it is she's trying to burn, desperately begging my mind not to provide me with the visual of it in use.

"*Dayam*, Nanna. Under normal circumstances that'd earn you a fist bump," George says, something like awe in his tone.

"*George...*" Web groans in warning.

George just shrugs, completely indifferent.

At that moment, the fire gives a sharp hiss and a loud pop and we all take a step back as the flames grow higher.

"Jesus, Nanna—are there batteries in that?" Web demands.

"The sales girl talked me into it!" she cries.

Shit. I scrub a hand over my face in exasperation. We need to get this fire out before it starts exploding out onto the grass. The last thing we need is to be responsible for starting a wildfire. Then Nanna really *might* be looking at charges.

The problem is, Nanna can be one stubborn woman when she's got her mind set on something, and right now she seems determined to see this sex toy burn.

Fortunately, George steps in with a distraction. "Hey, Nanna? How 'bout you and I go have a little chat. I want to ask you about something."

Nanna frowns at George for a moment before finally nodding and allowing him to guide her to the far corner of the yard, where there's a little bench situated under a large cherry tree. George might be completely ridiculous the vast majority of the time, but he's also one of those people that just oozes charm. He's got this entire town wrapped around his little finger, and our grandmother is no exception. It's hardly surprising to see her give in so easily to his suggestion.

"Fuck, this is insane," Web says as we take the opportunity to douse the fire. "Why didn't she just bury it?"

My brows shoot up. "Bury it? Dude, no one even knew she had it, and even if they did, no one would care. She could have just left it in one of her drawers, or thrown it out with the trash if she really didn't want it."

Web shrugs a shoulder. "Yeah, well, grief does funny things to people. And she's probably feeling pretty guilty, too, if he died while she was…y'know."

I let out a loud groan. "Dude… Not. Cool."

He huffs a quiet laugh. "Sorry."

I cast my gaze over to the back corner of the yard and see Nanna and George are still talking, and she seems to have calmed down; that cornered, frightened look she had when we arrived is completely gone. She's still not her usual sunny self, though, which is completely understandable.

"We should probably get rid of this before she comes back," Web suggests, nodding down at the silicone carcass, now covered in fire extinguisher foam.

I nod. "Yeah, good idea."

We both stand there for a moment, before Web gestures at me in encouragement. I stare at him incredulously. "You've got to be joking. I'm not picking it up. You do it."

His face screws up in distaste. "Hell no. I'm not touching that thing. You *know* where it's been." We glare at each other stubbornly for a long moment before Web lets out a heavy sigh, offering me an entreating look. "Come on, man. You touch guys asses all the time. This isn't that different."

My mouth falls open in horror, my voice going strangely high-pitched as I exclaim, "This is *very* different!"

"What's going on?"

I snap my head around to find George has approached without us realizing.

At my questioning look, he gestures behind him to where Nanna is still sitting on the bench. "She wanted to be alone for a bit. What are you idiots arguing about?"

Web waves a hand at the fire pit. "We need to get rid of

the strap-on before Nanna decides to try burning down Northern California again, but neither of us want to touch it."

George just rolls his eyes in exasperation and steps forward, plucking the crispy fried remains of the former strap-on from the fire pit without complaint. "You're both idiots," he mutters.

2

From the private Facebook group 'Finchley Locals Community Hangout'

Post by Bennett Goode: On behalf of all the Goodes we're saddened to announce the passing of a beloved husband, father, father-in-law, grandfather, and great-grandfather.
Edward (Ted) Goode passed in the early hours of Sunday morning after experiencing a heart attack late Saturday night. He was 79 years old and completely irreplaceable.
Beth Bowry reply to Bennett Goode's post: Such a tragedy. He'll be so missed *crying emoji*
Charlotte Rowe reply to Bennett Goode's post: Such sad news. You're all in my prayers *heart emoji*
George Goode reply to Bennett Goode's post: At least he died doing what he loved
Lorelai Goode reply to George Goode's comment: George! Have some sensitivity!
Nora Goode reply to Lorelai Goode's comment: Don't

chastise the boy Lorelai, I take it as a compliment *wink emoji*

Zack

Here's some free advice: don't ever date your boss. I don't care how charming he is, how amazingly he wears those designer suits, or how easily he can turn you on with one of his sexy smiles…

Just. Don't. Do. It.

And if, on the off chance, you decide to ignore my words of wisdom, here's another tip: when you walk in on your boyfriend slash boss balls deep inside Piedro, the nineteen-year-old intern, I urge you—nay, I beg you—to take the high road. Just walk out of there and don't look back. This asshole is not worth your tears or your anger or your ill-planned drunken retribution.

Perhaps if I'd taken this advice I could have avoided ending up in my current situation: sitting in a HR meeting, discussing my (non-existent) future at Burton Media while security footage of my best friend, Lawson, and me vandalizing Rick the Dick's office with shaving cream and toilet paper plays out on a laptop screen in front of me.

I bite my lower lip, deciding the only thing I can do is go for the Shaggy defense and pray they buy it. "That wasn't me."

Of course, that holds up for about two seconds before

I'm thwarted by Drunk Me on the laptop screen as I turn face-on to the camera and flip the double bird before folding over in laughter and then stumbling out the door, holding on to Lawson for support. Fuck. *Damn you, tequila!*

I look up at Anita Nelson, head of HR, to see her arching an eyebrow at me, as if challenging me to continue with my denials. I say nothing.

"We've managed to talk Rick out of filing charges," Anita tells me, "but he wants you gone. And seeing as how destruction of company property is a clear violation of company protocols..." she trails off, offering me a small shrug instead of the clichéd 'my hands are tied.'

This raises my hackles and I can practically feel the steam coming out of my ears. *Why don't you talk to Rick about company protocols?* I'm pretty sure banging an intern on his desk—with the door open, I might add—is a violation of fucking company protocols!

I don't say this out loud, of course; while I may have no interest in remaining employed at Burton Media, I do have an interest in being employed in general. And that prospect will require a reference from this woman. Ergo, it's time to kiss some serious ass.

By the time I leave Burton's downtown offices a half hour later, my small box of personal possessions lugged under one arm, I have absolutely no idea whether I've managed to recover any semblance of good standing. Despite my suspicions that Anita has long disliked Rick and—although she'd die before admitting it—seemed mildly amused at my prank, that's hardly enough to let me off the hook. I slept with my boss and then vandalized company property; for all I know, I'm about to be blacklisted from every media company in Chicago.

When I get on the L, I manage to find a seat between a middle-aged woman reading a book, and a teenager typing so fast on his phone it looks like his fingers are in danger of catching fire. I hold tighter to the small box I have precariously balanced on my lap and rest my head back against the window, mentally counting down the stops. All I want right now is to get home, change into some sweatpants, open a bottle of wine, and watch some reality TV.

I manage to hold back the groan that begs to escape when the Sam Smith song playing through my earphones is interrupted by Laura Branigan's "Gloria"—my mother's ringtone. I spend a brief moment debating whether to let the call go, but in the end I decide to answer; she'll only call back in five minutes' time if I don't.

"You couldn't have waited half an hour until I got home and opened a bottle of wine before you started in on how terrible my life is and how I should move back to Finchley?"

"A bottle of wine? Zack, it's ten in the morning!" Mom's tone is aghast.

"You're in California—I'm a whole two hours ahead of you here."

"That's still very concerning. I didn't raise you to be a lush."

I roll my eyes. "You barely raised me at all." I feel a stab of guilt the moment the comment leaves my lips, and I know the only reason I said it is because it's been such a shit couple days. Still, it's true...

Mom lets out a heavy breath before unloading her next words. "What should I have done? Worked less and let you boys starve? I wasn't the one who left, you know..."

"I know. I'm sorry, Mom. it's just been a really crappy few days and I lashed out."

Mom doesn't ask me for details. She knows it would be pointless anyway. We've just never really had the kind of relationship where I ask her for advice and talk about my problems. I know she wishes we were more like that, and maybe on some level I do as well, but this is the way we've always been. It's too late to change it now.

"I hate to pile on," she says after a long stretch of silence, "but I have some bad news."

"What is it?" I sit up straighter, immediately on guard. My first thought is for my brother, Jesse; he's a pediatric nurse in New York, and while I know he can more than take care of himself, I do worry sometimes about the long hours and the toll the job takes on him.

"It's Ted Goode. He...he passed away yesterday."

All the breath in my body rushes out as I try to process those words. It can't be true. It just can't be.

Ted is—or, I guess, was—the grandfather of my high school boyfriend, Slater. But he was so much more than that to me. We lived next door to the Goodes for as long as I can remember, and after my Dad left when I was seven, Ted stepped in and became the father I needed. He retired young—while in his early fifties—so while our mom was off scraping together a living, Ted and his wife, Nora—when she wasn't working her part-time bakery job—watched out for Jesse and me. They treated us just like two extra grandkids; and with thirteen of their own you'd think they'd have enough of kids running around. But they've always had a 'the more the merrier' attitude.

Despite the trauma of my dad taking off and the fact that I hardly ever saw my mom, my childhood was amazing, and it was all thanks to this man whom my mom is now telling me has passed away. And I haven't bothered to visit him for over five years...

"No." I finally manage to utter.

"I'm so sorry, honey." And I can tell my mom is on the verge of tears.

"How? What—what happened?" Ted was in his late seventies—not exactly old by today's standards—and as far as I knew, he'd been completely healthy.

"It was a...a heart attack," Mom tells me, but from the brief hesitation, I get the impression there's more to the story.

"What is it, Mom? What aren't you telling me?"

"Oh, Zack, I'm not sure you really want to know all the details."

"Just tell me, Mom—I'm a big boy."

She releases a heavy breath before speaking. "It seems they were...ahem...in the throes of passion when it happened. Ted and Nora, I mean."

I'm silent for a few moments as I attempt to compute her words. "You mean...he died during sex?"

Out of the corner of my eye I notice the woman next to me—the one reading the book that I now realize has a picture of an extremely attractive bare-chested man on the cover—jolt in alarm. *Eavesdrop much?*

"Err...yes," is Mom's awkward response. "At least, that's what they're saying around town. Apparently they were...trying something new and, well..." she trails off.

"You were right," I mumble. "I don't think I want the details."

After a brief pause, Mom said, "Honey, I have to go so I can call Jesse—he should be off work by now. Can I expect you home for the funeral? It's on Friday."

Shit. Finchley is the absolute last place I want to be right now considering the current mess that is my life, but there's no way I can skip out on paying my respects to Ted.

"Yeah," I say in a hoarse voice choked with emotion, "I'll be there."

When I end the call, the romance novel lady sitting next to me turns in my direction and says, "I'm so sorry, I couldn't help overhearing...you've lost someone?"

All I want to do right now is put Sam Smith back in my ears and curl up next to the wall of the train for the remaining twenty minutes of my journey home, so I'm a little annoyed that this stranger has decided to talk to me. I was raised to be polite, though, so I answer her in a stiff tone. "My grandfather." It would be way too difficult and completely unnecessary to explain my actual relationship with Ted.

"Oh, I'm so sorry, dear—that's awful."

The gentle tone and the genuine sympathy I see in her expression is what breaks me, and suddenly I'm reduced to a sobbing mess right here on the L, and I don't even have the energy to care about my public breakdown. "This is why old people shouldn't have sex. When old people have sex they die!"

"Now, that's just not true." Romance Novel Lady reaches to awkwardly rub my shoulder in what I'm guessing is supposed to be a soothing gesture. "Sex has been proven to have numerous health benefits—both mentally and physically."

Her comment is enough to startle me out of my outburst and I look up at her, eyes wide.

Perhaps taking my expression as disbelief at her words, rather than at the fact that she said them, she continues, "That's right. And if you're not having intercourse regularly, you really should be masturbating. Nothing better for a person's overall wellbeing than frequent orgasms."

Before I can muster a response to this, Romance Novel Lady glances up and gives a little jolt of surprise. "Oh, this is me." With one last squeeze of my shoulder, she says, "I am so sorry for your loss, dear," before getting to her feet and making her way to the exit of the train.

When I get home, I'm both annoyed and perturbed to find the front door of my apartment locked. It's this ridiculously ancient lock that takes a lot of finagling and concentration to open, so we only ever lock it when we're both out of the apartment. And considering it's just after midday, Lawson should be home right now.

After a good few minutes of wrestling with it, I finally manage to get the door unlocked, shoving it open with my shoulder and entering my apartment, my little box of personal items hugged under my arm.

I find Lawson standing in the middle of the living room wearing a startled expression, as if I've just caught him with his hand down his pants.

"What the fuck? Why was the door locked?" I demand.

But before the question is even out of my mouth, I've managed to deduce the answer based on Lawson's appearance and the state of the living room. He's shirtless, shoeless, his jeans are undone, and his normally neatly-styled black hair is an absolute mess. The living room floor is littered with items of male clothing: another pair of jeans, t-shirts, shoes…

I let out a huff of frustration and make my way over to the small kitchen, placing the box on the counter and slipping my messenger bag off my shoulder to set it on the floor. And that's when I see it: the naked man trying to hide behind the kitchen counter, as if crouching on his haunches and remaining silent will somehow make him invisible.

I round the counter and fix him with a bored glance, one eyebrow raised. "You had the whole five minutes it took me to open the door and this is where you chose to hide?"

Nervously, he gets to his feet, grabbing the dishtowel from the oven door to cover his crotchal area as he rises. He's cute. And very familiar…it takes me a moment to place him out of context, but then I realize he works at the coffee house just down the block. The one Lawson and I go to almost every day. And as far as I recall, he has a girlfriend.

"I thought you said no one would be home." He casts a panicked look in Lawson's direction.

I turn toward my best friend, fixing him with an incredulous look. "Really? You didn't think after our little escapade on Friday night I might not last the whole day?"

His face screws up in sympathy. "Fuck, man, I'm sorry." Turning to barista boy, he says, "Listen, Toby, you don't need to worry about Zack, he's cool."

Barista Boy—Toby—studies me warily. "He doesn't seem cool."

Aaannnd I snap. "Yeah, well, my boyfriend cheated on me with a nineteen-year-old named Piedro, I lost my job, my grandfather died, and then I came home with the sole intention of drinking three bottles of wine to find a naked barista in my kitchen!"

Toby's eyes widen in shock and he takes a small step back, obviously to get as much distance from the crazy man as possible. With a brief glance toward Lawson, he says, "Umm, I think I might go."

"That's a good idea," I say. "And for the love of god, please take that dishtowel with you."

3

From the private Facebook group 'Finchley Locals Community Hangout'

Post by Hank Latham: On behalf of all Finchley residents I'd like to express my sincere regrets about the passing of Ted Goode. He was a great man and he'll be missed. Also, does this mean there's a vacancy on the Men's Club board?

Alice Ackerman reply to Hank Latham's post: Well unless there's a way for Ted to chair the board from the beyond I would assume the answer is yes, but this is hardly the time to be discussing such matters Hank

Hank Latham reply to Alice Ackerman's comment: This is a matter for the Men's Club, Alice. Which you are not a member of

Alice Ackerman reply to Hank Latham's comment: Then post it in the Finchley Men's Club Facebook group

Zack

When Lawson leaves to walk Toby out, I make a beeline for the shower, soaking myself under the scalding hot spray for a good twenty minutes.

Afterward, I return to the living room, dressed in my oldest, comfiest sweatpants and a Sacramento Kings jersey. I'm just flopping onto the couch, remote in hand, when Lawson steps through the front door carrying a large paper bag. It only takes one glance at the logo on the bag for all my annoyance at his earlier behavior to completely evaporate; he's brought me parmesan fries from the pizza place two doors down—my favorite food on the planet.

He joins me on the sofa, spreading the take out boxes on the coffee table. As well as two servings of parmesan fries, he's also brought home a serving of chicken fingers and some mozzarella sticks. Bless him.

"Wine. I need wine," I tell him.

He chuckles. "I'm pretty sure we drank all the wine on Friday before we started on the tequila."

I groan. "You've *got* to be kidding me."

"Hang on, I'll check." Lawson pulls himself up off the couch and pads toward the kitchen.

I twist around in my seat so I can watch as he searches through the fridge, eventually excavating what appears to be a six-pack of something.

"This is all we have," he says.

"What is it?"

"Pear cider."

I shrug. "It'll do."

I shift back around in my seat and use the remote to bring up one of our favorite shows: *Real Vegas Weddings*.

"Are these new or old?" Lawson asks, nodding to the TV.

"Old. I'm pretty sure this is the one where the bride punched Elvis and then threw up all over the groom."

Lawson lets out a loud rumble of laughter. "Oh my god, I hope so. That was an awesome one!"

We sit there eating and drinking for about half an episode before I bring up the scene from earlier.

"Law, you can't keep doing this—the whole 'seducing the straight guy' routine, I mean. It's not healthy." My tone is weary; this is a conversation we've had many times.

"They're not straight," he clarifies. "They're bi-curious. Otherwise they wouldn't be hooking up with me."

I roll my eyes. "Well they identify as straight. I know this is your clever way of avoiding commitment, but aren't you at least a little worried about the kind of doubt and confusion you're inflicting on these guys?"

"Hey! It's not like I'm forcing anyone to do anything they don't want to do." Casting me a narrowed glance, he says, "How about we stop with the judgment? You don't see me calling you out on your poor romantic choices."

I huff a rueful laugh. "Oh, please. You told me frequently what a bad idea you thought my dating Rick was."

He shrugs one broad shoulder. "I was right, wasn't I?"

I slump back against the couch, completely deflated. "Yeah. You were."

Forgetting he was pissed at me two seconds ago, Lawson sits back beside me, his shoulder resting against mine. "So, he fired you?" he asks gently.

I sigh. "Well, technically HR fired me. But, yeah, it came from him."

"What are you going to do now?"

I take a generous sip of my cider before answering. "I have no idea. Look for another job, I guess. But that could be impossible. For all I know, every media company in Chicago already knows I slept with my boss and then trashed his office. No one is going to want to hire that hot mess."

Lawson reaches out to grab a mozzarella stick, chewing it thoughtfully. I can see his mind is turning something over so I merely take another sip of my cider and wait for him to speak. Finally, he says, "Why don't you work for me?"

"What?"

He shrugs. "You could handle all my social media. And my website. And you could run my ads for me. You know I hate doing all that stuff, and you're really good at it. And I'm earning enough now that I can pay someone to do it for me." He shrugs again. "May as well be the person who knows me best."

I consider him for a moment, my expression doubtful. Lawson is a self-published author who writes gay spy thrillers—kind of a what if Jack Ryan was secretly gay and involved in a heated affair with a married MI-6 agent? premise—you'd be amazed at how popular they are. They're the kind of books no major publishing company would touch, but thanks to self-publishing he's been able to gather something of a cult following and earn a pretty good living for himself. He's not rolling around in cash by any means, but he's doing a lot better than the majority of authors—both traditionally and self-published—out there. Even with his success, though, I'm not sure how feasible this would be in terms of a career move for me. "It's a nice idea, Law, but I'm not sure you'd have enough work for me to do it full-time. And even if you can afford to pay me, you couldn't cover my entire salary. I'm used to doing that kind of work for dozens of people at a time."

"Okay, so you start off with just me. And it could either be a way to keep you busy and tide you over until you find something else...or I could be the first client for your new company..."

I stare at him, wide-eyed. *My own company...*I've thought about it, of course, but it's always seemed like a bit of a pipe dream. It still does, to be honest. I always assumed by the time I was ready to go out on my own I'd have made more of a name for myself and have a bunch of clients who'd be willing to come with me...if I started something new now, it would be completely from scratch.

But it wouldn't be the worst idea to take him up on the suggestion to handle his marketing stuff until I find something new. It would at least make me feel like I'm working, rather than just bumming around like a schlub as I wait for job opportunities. "What would you need me to do?" I ask, warming to the idea.

"Well, just what I said. Social media, ad copy...that kind of thing. Just think of me as any other client—a client who doesn't have the time to manage their own website and stuff, just like all the ones you wrote copy for at Burton."

I think about it for a moment, biting my lower lip as I weigh the pros and cons. Who knows? It could be fun… and I could definitely help build Lawson's brand…and maybe after a few months he could provide me with a glowing reference that could open up new job possibilities?

Finally, I cast him a bright smile. "Okay."

"Yeah, you'll do it?"

"On a temporary basis." I have to be smart about this; Lawson might be able to afford a media manager right now, but that doesn't mean that will always be the case. And I know that if we agreed to some kind of permanent contract he'd feel obligated to keep me on even if he was no longer in the position to afford me.

We clink our bottles together to seal the deal.

"So…Ted's gone?" he asks, bringing the mood down dramatically.

I let out a heavy sigh, nodding my confirmation. "Mom called on my way home from work."

"What happened?"

I explain everything my mom told me, including the part about Ted and Nora being in bed together when the heart attack happened.

At my words, Lawson's eyes light up. "I can use this—a character dying in the throes of passion? That's gold." He stands up and starts pacing the room. I can practically see his imagination whirring, brewing up this new idea.

I should be offended that he wants to use Ted's death in this way, but I'm not; if anything, I think it'll be good if

Clean Slate 39

something creative can come out of this tragedy. And Ted would be laughing his ass off at the idea of providing the source of inspiration for one of Lawson's gay spy novels.

"Just imagine it," Lawson says, holding out his hands as if to paint a picture, "Drake Porter is in bed with someone he shouldn't be—maybe an enemy agent—and the guy dies while they're…y'know. Given the circumstances, Drake's obviously the top suspect, so he has to prove his innocence to the enemy government while also redeeming himself in the eyes of the United States by saving the world once again."

I furrow my brow in confusion. "Why is Drake sleeping with an enemy agent? What happened to Agent Scott?"

Lawson waves a dismissive hand. "They're on the outs because Scott won't leave his wife even though he's clearly in love with Drake—which makes it all the more interesting when Drake calls him for help."

I have to admit I'm impressed with how quickly Lawson pulled that together. It obviously needs a lot of work, but I have no doubt it'll be best-seller material by the time he's done with it.

I flash him a bright smile. "I think you might be onto another winner here."

Lawson returns my smile before slumping back down on the couch. We sit in a comfortable silence for a few moments before he reaches out to rub a gentle hand over my knee. "You know, when you think about it, it's actually kind of sweet."

"What is?"

"The way Ted died—making love with his wife. That

seems like pretty much the perfect way to leave this world, if you ask me…in the arms of the love of your life."

I'm quiet for a moment as I mull over his words. As much as I'd prefer not to think about Ted and Nora doing it, I can't deny Lawson makes a pretty good point.

I toss my head back against the sofa, glancing up at my best friend. "I think you might be right—it's exactly how Ted would have wanted to go. Well, either having sex or watching the Giants win the World Series…one of those."

"So," Lawson says after a long moment of silence, "you're going back?"

"Yeah—I have to say goodbye to him."

"When?"

I shrug one shoulder. "The funeral's on Friday, apparently, so I guess I'll fly out Thursday."

"I think you should go tomorrow."

"What? No." I spring up and fix him with an incredulous look. "I'm not spending any more time there than I have to."

Lawson sighs. "Z, don't you think you owe him more than just a flying visit? You should take a few days at least, spend some time with Nora—this can't be an easy time for her. I think that's what Ted would want."

I narrow my eyes. "You've never even met Ted. Or Nora."

"True," he says with a soft quirk of his lips, "but you talk about them so much I feel like I have." He fixes me with a stern look. "You know I'm right."

Throwing my head back against the couch, I let out a loud groan. Because he is.

4

From the private Facebook group 'Finchley Locals Community Hangout'

Post by Charlotte Rowe: Due to recent events, the Knitting and Book Club will be taking a break from our usual content. We'll be delving into a selection of British and American classics instead. Suggestions are welcome!

George Goode reply to Charlotte Rowe's post: WHAT? No!

Beth Bowry reply to Charlotte Rowe's post: But I've already finished that Sylvia Day book. I was looking forward to chatting about it *sad emoji*

George Goode reply to Beth Bowry's comment: Come into the bar anytime Mrs. B, we can chat about Gia and Jax *flame emoji* *flame emoji*

Alice Ackerman reply to Charlotte Rowe's post: Do many British or American classics have naughty bits in them? I like the books with naughty bits in them

Eloise Goode reply to Alice Ackerman's comment: I'll start googling and see what I can find

Beth Bowry reply to Charlotte Rowe's post: What about Bridgerton? Those books are set in England and there's sex in them!

Eloise Goode reply to Beth Bowry's comment: Ooh yes! Let's read Bridgerton!

Charlotte Rowe reply to Beth Bowry's comment: Well the point was to take a break from the sexy stuff after what happened to Ted...

Gloria Cartwright reply to Charlotte Rowe's post: What about Outlander? That's a classic!

Charlotte Rowe reply to Gloria Cartwright's comment: Again, kind of missing the point of the post. I was thinking more along the lines of Oliver Twist.

George Goode reply to Charlotte Rowe's comment: Boring!

Missy Clarke reply to Charlotte Rowe's post: I don't understand, what did Ted's death have to do with book club?

Harriett Goode reply to Missy Clarke's comment: I think the cat might be out of the bag...

Missy Clarke reply to Harriett Goode's comment: What cat? What am I missing?

Tansie Goode reply to Missy Clarke's comment: Well...it turns out Granddad's heart attack happened while he and Nanna were being intimate.

Tansie Goode reply to Missy Clarke's comment: There was prostate stimulation involved.

Tansie Goode reply to Missy Clarke's comment: Please don't make me go into more detail!

Clean Slate 43

George Goode reply to Missy Clarke's comment: *They were using a strap-on*

Harriett Goode reply to George Goode's comment: *George! Nanna didn't want everyone knowing about that!*

George Goode reply to Harriett Goode's comment: *It's Finchley. They'll all find out anyway *shrug emoji**

Charlotte Rowe reply to Missy Clarke's comment: *We can only assume Nora got the idea from some of the recent books we've been reading. I can't tell you how guilty I've been feeling since I found out *tear drop emoji**

Missy Clarke reply to Tansie Goode's comment: **shocked emoji* Oh my goodness! I never realized the prostate was such a dangerous part of the body! What about Gunner? Should I be worried? I want to encourage him to be himself but not if it's going to kill him!*

George Goode reply to Missy Clarke's comment: *Relax, Mrs. C. It was a freak accident. Prostate stimulation isn't dangerous, I promise.*

George Goode reply to Missy Clarke's comment: *Besides, you don't have to worry about Gunner anyway. I have it on good authority he's a top.*

Missy Clarke reply to George Goode's comment: *A top? What does that mean?*

George Goode reply to Missy Clarke's comment: *You know, I don't think he'd want me explaining it to you.*

Tansie Goode reply to George Goode's comment: *How do you even know? Have you slept with him?*

***George Goode* reply to *Tansie Goode*'s comment:** *Of course not. Things just come out on guys trips*

***Tansie Goode* reply to *George Goode*'s comment:** *How come I'm never invited to these guys trips?*

***George Goode* reply to *Tansie Goode*:** *I thought the answer to that would be pretty obvious, dear cousin*

***George Goode* reply to *Charlotte Rowe*'s comment:** *Don't feel bad, Char. Granddad's heart gave out. If it wasn't this that caused it it would have been something else. At least this way he got to go out with a bang!*

***Harriett Goode* reply to *George Goode*'s comment:** *GEORGE! Seriously! *Face palm emoji**

***George Goode* reply to *Harriett Goode*'s comment:** **Shrug emoji* Just telling it like it is, sis*

SLATER

SOMETHING that I perhaps should have already mentioned about my family is that it's huge. And with a couple of exceptions, the lot of us have been living in Finchley and it's surrounds ever since my great-grandmother, who'd been widowed during the second world war, met a nice barber named Jack at a county fair in 1949 and decided to move here with her nine-year-old son—my grandfather, Ted—so she and Jack could be married. Then, in the early sixties, my granddad met and married the love of his life: my grandmother, Nora, who happens to be pretty much my favorite person on the planet.

When Nanna's not freaking out and lighting the backyard on fire in her mission to be rid of unwanted sex toys —which is, fortunately, most of the time—she's pretty chill, and has a progressive view on life that's definitely rubbed off on all of us. Unlike my mom's asshole parents, Nanna didn't turn her back when my uncle Carson— George's dad—came home one day at the age of sixteen to tell her he'd gotten his girlfriend pregnant; she and Granddad just welcomed my aunt Lorelai into the family and doted on my cousin Candace when she was born. Of course, I wasn't actually there for all this, but I've heard the stories.

Apparently, the unexpected pregnancy did spur Nanna into sitting all four of her sons down—including my uncle Rock, who was only eight at the time—and giving them a lecture about responsible sex. Although it couldn't have worked all that well considering it was only a few years later that my dad brought my mom home, four months pregnant with my brother. But just like with Lorelai, Nanna and Granddad welcomed Mom with open arms.

Now it's over three decades later, and between my dad, Uncle Carson, and Uncle Bennett there are thirteen of us grandkids. And thanks to Candace and my sister Everley there are now a few midgets running around as well. Like I said—we're a big family.

And right now, we're all gathered at my parents' place to discuss details for Granddad's funeral on Friday.

"Did you guys *really* need to tell the whole town how Granddad died?" my cousin Delia asks in an exasperated tone, directing her question at George and my sister Tansie. Those two are around the same age and have been pretty much thick as thieves for as long as I remember—in other words, they're pretty much as bad as each other when it comes to getting into mischief.

"They all already knew anyway," George says with a shrug.

"And Charlotte wanted to cancel book club!" Tansie cries.

"Well, technically she just wanted to make book club boring, but that would have been the death knell," George clarifies.

"I have to agree," Mom says. "No one wanted to read *Oliver Twist*."

I roll my eyes. "Can we please get back to the plans for Friday?"

"Okay, who wants burgers?" my dad calls, coming in from outside carrying a tray of freshly-grilled burgers that smell absolutely delicious. "Pop, I've got some vegie ones here for you," he says with a nod to my cousin Poppy—the youngest of George's five older sisters.

"They don't have any dairy or other animal products in them, do they?" Poppy asks.

Dad pauses in his tracks for a moment. "No...?" Everyone in the room, including Poppy, can tell he has absolutely no idea whether the burgers are vegan or not.

Before Delia can make a fuss, I step in. "They're fine. We got them from Joey's."

Poppy lets out a little sigh, seeming placated. Joey is our local butcher and, like my dad, he doesn't seem to get the difference between veganism and vegetarianism. To be on the safe side, he just makes all his meatless 'meat' without any animal products whatsoever.

My dad sets the burgers down on the counter next to where Mom's set up a bunch of salad and buns and condiments and we all dive on the food as though we haven't eaten for days.

"Why don't we just do this?" My cousin Livia—yet another of George's many sisters—suggests as we're all scarfing down our burgers.

I glance up from helping Ethan clean up the coleslaw that's fallen out of the bottom of his bun. "Do what?"

"For Friday. Why don't we just do a grill—after the church service, obviously. We could just have it here. Burgers, ribs, that sort of thing," Livia clarifies.

We're all quiet for a moment as we glance around at each other, taking in the suggestion. Eventually, it's Nanna who has the final word. "That sounds perfect."

5

From the private Facebook group 'Finchley Locals Community Hangout'

Post by George Goode: Since Charlotte's gone and made the Knitting and Book Club boring, I'm starting a new Drinking and Book Club. Anyone who still wants to read dirty books can come by the saloon at 8pm Tuesdays and we'll drink and talk books

Alice Ackerman reply to George Goode's post: Will the drinks be free?

George Goode reply to Alice Ackerman's comment: I'm running a business here Mrs. A.

Alice Ackerman reply to George Goode's comment: Charlotte always gives us free drinks.

George Goode reply to Alice Ackerman's comment: *eye roll emoji* Water and instant coffee I can do. I'll even throw in free soda. But alcohol's at bar prices

Tansie Goode reply to George Goode's comment: Even for me?

GEORGE GOODE REPLY TO TANSIE GOODE'S COMMENT: WHEN WAS THE LAST TIME YOU PAID FOR A DRINK AT THE SALOON, FREELOADER?

ALICE ACKERMAN REPLY TO GEORGE GOODE'S POST: CAN WE STILL KNIT?

BETH BOWRY REPLY TO ALICE ACKERMAN'S COMMENT: WHAT ARE YOU KNITTING IN JULY??

ALICE ACKERMAN REPLY TO BETH BOWRY'S COMMENT: FIFI GETS COLD SITTING UNDER THE A/C

GEORGE GOODE REPLY TO ALICE ACKERMAN'S COMMENT: YES MRS. A, YOU CAN STILL KNIT *WINK EMOJI*

BETH BOWRY REPLY TO ALICE ACKERMAN'S COMMENT: OR YOU COULD JUST SHUT THE A/C OFF AND HELP SAVE THE PLANET *SHRUG EMOJI*

Zack

"Oh my god, I can't do this," I say into the rental car's Bluetooth system as I cross the American River, the landmark that tells me I'm only about fifteen miles out from Finchley.

"Yes, you can, Zack," Lawson's disembodied voice says in a stern tone.

"You don't know what it's like in small towns like these, Law. What am I supposed to tell everyone when they ask me about my job?"

"That's easy. Tell them you're the social media manager for a best-selling author. It's the truth."

"As of yesterday."

"They don't need to know that part."

"And what about when they ask me about my love life?"

"There's nothing wrong with being single, Z."

"I know that," I say with a soft groan. "It's just, if I'm single and he's single the whole town is going to be expecting us to get back together. I'm not sure I can deal with that pressure right now."

"I see…and what if he's not single."

Oh my god. I hadn't even thought of that! "Oh my god. I hadn't even thought of that!" I repeat out loud. "Lawson, there's no way I can show up there alone if he's in a committed fucking relationship! I can't be the loser in this break up!" Sure, it was twelve years ago, but for some reason every time I return to Finchley I feel like it was yesterday.

"Hell no! No way are you the loser in this break up. You got me didn't you?"

I let out a wry chuckle. "Yeah, I guess I did."

"Well, there's your victory right there." There's a beat of comfortable silence before Lawson says, "Z? I think this is something you need to deal with this time. Don't avoid him like you did last time you were there. Or the time before that. Or the time before that…"

"I get it, Law," I say irritably, wishing for once he didn't remember every freakin' detail. *Authors.*

"Just…talk to him," he suggests, his tone a little gentler. "Hash it out. Then you can move on."

"I've moved on." My tone is full of indignation.

"No," he says firmly, "you've run away. That's not the same thing."

Urgh. I hate when he's right.

When I arrive at my mom's place, I'm not entirely surprised to find she's not home. Despite no longer needing to support Jesse and me, she still works the same long hours at the county hospital that she used to.

I'm just walking up the drive, tugging my suitcase along behind me when I hear a friendly voice calling out. "Oh my god. That can't be Zack Cartwright?"

I spin around, finding myself facing one of the many members of the Goode family; I suppose I shouldn't be surprised considering they make up a decent chunk of the town's population. And the fact that their grandmother lives next door to my mom definitely increases the odds.

I smile politely at the woman rushing over to me from Nora's front yard. At first I think it's Slater's aunt Lorelai, but then I remember she must be in her fifties by now, and this woman is early thirties at most. It must be one of Lorelai's daughters.

I do a quick inventory of what I remember about the five girls as I try to figure out who this is; I feel terrible that she's recognized me instantly but I'm having such a hard time with her. I rule out Candace straight away—she was always tiny and this woman is at least five eight or nine, almost as tall as I am. I remember the two younger ones—Delia and Poppy—always looked a lot more like their dad than their mom…so this must be one of the twins. Great.

Growing up, there was only one way I could ever tell the difference between Livia and Harriet, and as she approaches I'm just praying that hasn't changed. Fortunately, as she gets closer I can see the crooked right incisor clear as day as she smiles at me.

I let out a small breath of relief. "Hey, Livia, how's it going?"

"Not bad. It's been a tough week but we're getting through it."

I nod sadly. "I'm so sorry about Ted."

"Thanks. You know, I've got to say, I'm a little surprised to see you here."

My brows shoot up. "You didn't think I'd come back for this?"

"No, no, that's not what I meant," she says with a wave of her hand. "I just figured you'd come for the funeral. That's what your brother's doing, right? I wasn't expecting to see you this early."

"I had some time off work," I hedge, offering a small shrug. "I thought it'd be good to come back a bit early, spend some time with Nora…"

Livia smiles. "That's really sweet of you. I'm sure she'll appreciate it."

We chat for a little longer and she updates me with a few tidbits about the family and details for the funeral and wake on Friday. She also mentions she's now running a little boutique and invites me to come check it out.

"I'll be there this afternoon if you want to stop by," she offers.

I nod. "Thanks, sounds great."

We leave it there and she heads back across to Nora's, while I head inside Mom's house. I let out a heavy sigh as I cross the threshold of the front door. Every time I come back here to stay—which, admittedly, isn't that often—I feel like I'm being transported back to my teenage years. It's an odd feeling—part nostalgia, part bitterness.

I drag my suitcase through the hall and then up the stairs to the bedroom I lived in until I left for college. It's exactly the same as it's always been. Not because of any kind of sentimental attachment on Mom's part; it's just that she's always been too busy and distracted to deal with packing it up. And I guess there's never really been a need.

I open my suitcase and unpack all my stuff, re-folding all my clothes neatly and finding places for everything in my old closet and dresser. If there's one thing I loathe, it's living out of a suitcase. After I'm done unpacking, I grab a change of clothes and head to the bathroom for a shower to wash the day's travel away.

Once I'm refreshed, I head down to the kitchen for a quick bite to eat before deciding to take Livia up on her suggestion to visit her boutique. I'll have to face the town at some point so I may as well rip the Band-Aid off now.

If you saw it from the air, Finchley's town center would look kind of like a stick figure drawing with no arms or legs. It basically consists of one long main street with a small park at the end of it and a circuit of shops and businesses wrapped around the park on the opposite side of the road. The town was founded in the 1800s during the gold rush, and between the balconied buildings on Main Street, the old-timey saloon, the soda shoppe, and the horse and carriage currently clomping around the town, it definitely gives visitors the feeling of stepping into a time machine. Of course, for me it feels more like stepping back into my childhood, rather than all the way to the 1800s, but it's a strange feeling nonetheless.

I've only been back here a few times since I left for college twelve years ago and it always feels the same. Probably because the town hardly ever changes...

I find Livia's boutique pretty easily; she mentioned it was opposite the park, a couple doors down from the library, so getting my bearings isn't difficult. As I pass the library, I notice a couple other changes to the town: the small medical practice that used to be here next to the tourist info center has disappeared, replaced by a restaurant that I'm *definitely* going to have to check out; and next to that, the little pet store has now been turned into a wine and cheese bar. I make another mental note to check that out while I'm here.

The place Livia has secured for her boutique used to be an antique store, and considering there are two others already in the town, it doesn't surprise me she decided to do something different once she took over the lease.

I step inside and am immediately greeted with a bright smile, but it's Harriett who I encounter this time. And, unlike this morning, I can tell instantly because, having seen Livia so recently, their differences couldn't be more stark. Harriett's hair is now a lighter color and cut in a different style, and she's curvier than her twin—not that that takes away from her attractiveness at all. Objectively speaking, obviously.

"Livvy told me you might be coming by!" Harriett exclaims excitedly. "It's so good to see you!"

I grin at her. The twins were a year above me and Slater at school, but I always got along with them really well. They were like a couple of older sisters, really. "You too. This place looks great—are you running it too?"

She shakes her head. "I work at the library but I help out if Livia needs me."

I nod, offering a soft smile. "That's awesome. I just walked past the library, actually. What happened to all the places along there? The doctor's and the pet store?" I ask curiously, before adding, "Not that I'm complaining that there's more than one place to eat out in this town now."

Harriett chuckles. "Well, June Oster decided to pack up and move away after her husband passed, so she sold the pet store. There was definitely a lot of grumbling when the new owners decided to close it down and turn it into a wine bar, but people got over it—everyone gets pet supplies online now anyway," she adds with a shrug. "And Dr. Bailey moved to the new clinic a few years ago, so the doctor's offices got sold as well."

Huh. I had no idea there was a new clinic, which is weird because with my mom being a nurse, you'd think that's something she'd tell me. I guess she figured I wouldn't be that interested...

I end up spending the whole afternoon at the boutique catching up with Harriett and then Livia when she arrives later in the day. It's not until they're closing up for the day that I realize just how much time I've spent there, and that I'm absolutely starving.

Livia chuckles as my stomach lets out a loud grumble

just as we're leaving the boutique. "Come on, lets go get you something to eat before you fall over faint."

I start to protest that I'm fine, but they each grab one of my arms and link elbows with me, steering me in the direction of Main Street.

They take me to the saloon, which is *so* not where I planned to eat dinner on my first night back in town, but my options are limited, and I am getting pretty freakin' starving.

Once inside, we make a beeline for one of the booths and shuffle in. I snatch a paper flier from the table, assuming it's the menu, but as I read I realize I'm mistaken.

"What's this?" I ask, frowning in puzzlement.

Harriett glances over my shoulder for a second. "Oh, that's something George has cooked up. He was upset that Charlotte wanted to stop doing dirty books for book club so he's started his own."

"Apparently they're reading one of the *Bridgerton* books tonight," Livia pipes in.

Harriett nods. "Yep. And Alice Ackerman's going to do a dramatic reading."

I stare at her for a moment, not entirely sure how to process all of that. Finally, I manage to ask, "Mrs. Ackerman? Our high school drama teacher?"

Harriett nods. "Yep. So I imagine it will be very...lively."

I shake my head in baffled amazement before glancing down at the flier again. "I thought George was off on an oil rig or something?"

Livia lets out a tinkling laugh. "Oh, honey, you are

majorly out of the loop! He came back years ago after dad had that heart scare. He owns this place now."

My mouth falls open in shock. "*George Goode* owns the Finchley Saloon?"

Livia and Harriett both chuckle, neither of them the least bit insulted on behalf of their brother.

Harriett says something, but I don't quite hear her. It feels like every sound in the room has been drowned out by the blood rushing in my ears as my heart starts pumping a million miles an hour. Slater Goode has just walked into the saloon. And he looks fucking incredible.

I'm *so* not ready for this…

6

From the private Facebook group 'Finchley Locals Community Hangout'

Post by Missy Clarke: Does the Knitting and Drinking and Book Club meeting start at 8pm or 9pm tonight?
Beth Bowry reply to Missy Clarke's post: 8pm. Scroll down, the info's on George's post below!

Slater

"What the fuck are you eating?"

"What does it look like?" I say, holding up the cling-wrapped, pre-toasted Pop Tart for Web to inspect, before taking a bite and talking with my mouth full of sugary, fruity—albeit cold and slightly soggy—goodness. "It's a Pop Tart."

Web just shakes his head in bemusement. "What are you, seven? Why did you pack pre-toasted Pop Tarts for lunch?"

We've just sat down on the bed of my truck to dig into our lunch. It's a beautiful day; the sun is beating down, but there's a nice breeze that's keeping the worst of the heat at bay.

I swallow my bite and give a small shrug of one shoulder. "Only thing we had in the house. With everything that's been going on I haven't had a chance to get groceries—the situation is dire, man."

Web takes a bite of his sandwich and yeah, I've got to admit, I'm having some serious food envy right now, 'cause that thing looks amazing.

"Why couldn't Chance do it?"

I shake my head. "Oh no, Chance is way too busy right now—did you know Mrs. Henderson is suing her cat again?"

A bright grin cracks through the thick layer of dark scruff covering Web's face and he lets out a rumbling chuckle. "Nope, I must've missed that scoop." He shoots me a questioning glance. "So, do I take it you'll be hitting the saloon for dinner tonight?"

I nod. "Yep. But I have every intention of being out of there well before this book reading thing of George's starts."

Web's brows shoot up. "Is there actually going to be a reading?"

I shrug. "I have no fucking clue. All I know is my

mom's going to be there talking about dirty books and I *so* don't need to be witness to that."

After lunch, Web and I get back to work installing the custom-made staircase Web's made for our client. With me being a carpenter and him being a joiner, it makes sense for us to refer clients to each other and we often find ourselves working on jobs together. It's led to us making the decision to merge our businesses and keep everything in the one place; it's something we've been talking about for a while, but now it's actually happening and we should be making it official pretty soon.

When we're done with work for the day, we each go home to freshen up and agree to meet later at the saloon for some dinner. I probably shouldn't be eating out *again*, and instead be spending the time collecting some groceries and making a nice, healthy dinner at home; but it's been a long day and I just want some good food right now. Plus, I get a pretty good discount at the Finchley Saloon because George runs the place.

When I walk into the saloon a little while later, I'm hit with a strange, prickling sensation that runs through my whole body. And when I glance around, I realize why. Zack Cartwright—my high school boyfriend and the love of my life—is sitting at a booth with two of my cousins, and he's staring right at me, his expression a mix of dread and awe that I can't remotely begin to figure out.

I'm completely rooted to the spot, just inside the door, and I can't stop myself from staring right back as a wave of memories and not-so-deeply-buried feelings comes rushing at me.

Damn, he looks good. My gut does a kind of nervous,

flip-flopping thing as I take everything in: from the penetrating gray gaze, to the neatly-styled dark hair, to the day's worth of stubble covering his angular jaw. He's wearing a pale blue and white striped t-shirt that fits perfectly over his lean frame and emphasizes his golden tan.

I let out a long, shaky breath as I finally manage to tear my gaze away and walk over to the bar on unsteady legs. It's not like I forgot how gorgeous he was, but seeing it in person compared to in a memory is just a completely different situation.

When I get to the bar, George quickly wraps up a conversation he's having with another customer and bustles over to greet me. "He's here for the funeral," he says, taking out a glass and pouring a beer from the tap for me.

"I figured."

"Are you going to talk to him?" George asks, sliding the beer across the bar to me.

"And say what?"

He arches a brow at me. "I don't know. I guess you could start with 'Hey, how's it going?' and then work in the bit about you still being completely in love with him."

"*Shhh*," I hiss angrily, cutting off any more of that line of talking. "This town gossips enough as it is."

"If you ask me it doesn't gossip enough," George says with a smirk.

I shake my head in exasperation and take a sip of my beer. Web and Axel join us not long after that and we all order some food.

Throughout the dinner, although I'm managing to

keep up with the others' conversation, I'm incredibly conscious of Zack on the other side of the room. He, Livia, and Harriett have been joined by my sister Tansie and the four of them seem to be having a grand old time, with Ella—one of the saloon's servers—returning to their table again and again to refill wine glasses.

"I hope you boys are planning to stay for Knitting and Drinking and Book Club," George says after we're done with out food.

Web, Axel, and I exchange doubtful glances. "Yeah, I don't think so," I say on behalf of all three of us. "It doesn't really sound like our thing."

"Since when is drinking and talking about sex not your thing?" George asks.

"Since it involves a dramatic reading by Mrs. Ackerman and my mom's presence," Axel supplies.

Web nods. "What he said."

George just shrugs. "Okay, but you boys are missing out. It's going to be epic."

Somehow I doubt 'epic' is the right adjective for a book reading, but whatever. "I'll take the risk," I say.

Before we leave, I make a quick stop at the bathroom. And as I'm heading back down the hallway, I run smack into someone, almost sending them toppling over but managing to reach out and steady them in time.

Glancing up, I realize the person I've got a hold of is Zack. I'm frozen in place again as I just stare at him for a long moment, but then I finally manage to pull my hands away and take a step back. "Sorry."

"Why do you look like that?" he demands, clearly agitated.

My brows draw together in confusion and I glance down at my appearance. Nothing seems to be amiss; I'm just in jeans and a plain white t-shirt. "Like what?"

"Like *that!*" He says again, waving a hand about in frustration. "All perfect and golden, and not at all bald. Or fat. Or covered in disfiguring boils of any kind."

My brows shoot up in question. "Umm…"

"You're supposed to be hideous! *That's* the rule!"

"It is?"

"Yes! Don't you know *anything?*" And with that frustrated comment, he gives an aggravated huff and pushes past me into the restroom.

I stand there for a moment, completely baffled; he's clearly drunker than I realized earlier…

It's not until much later, well after I've gotten home, that I realize exactly how drunk Zack got tonight, though. I'm in bed and almost asleep when I hear my phone vibrating on my nightstand.

George Goode: *Dude! Your boy is wasted! He just spewed all over Mabel!*

Me: *The horse?*

George Goode: *Yup! Right on the ass *laugh emoji**

7

From the private Facebook group 'Finchley Locals Community Hangout'

Post by Raymond 'Sheriff' Taylor: Locals should be made aware of an incident that occurred last night between the hours of nine and ten pm outside Finchley Saloon. Hank Latham has made a report that Mabel was assaulted by an unknown drunken lout. Everyone should be on the lookout for unsavory characters in the area.

Beth Bowry reply to Raymond 'Sheriff' Taylor's post: Mabel? You mean the horse?

Raymond 'Sheriff' Taylor reply to Beth Bowry's comment: Yes. Apparently she's traumatized, the poor thing.

Beth Bowry reply to Raymond 'Sheriff' Taylor's comment: It's a horse

Raymond 'Sheriff' Taylor reply to Beth Bowry's comment: Horses have feelings too, Elizabeth

Harriett Goode reply to Raymond 'Sheriff' Taylor's post: Your drunken lout is Zack Cartwright *laugh emoji*

Missy Clarke reply to Harriett Goode's comment: I thought Zack lived in Canada?

Harriet Goode reply to Missy Clarke's comment: Chicago. He's back for the funeral.

Hank Latham reply to Harriett Goode's comment: So he says. But first opportunity he gets, he takes advantage of my Mabel! Rotten to the core, that one. I always knew it.

Alice Ackerman reply to Hank Latham's comment: Don't be crazy. Zack's a good boy.

Missy Clarke reply to Harriett Goode's comment: Do you think now that Zack's back he and Slater will get back together? I love a good reunion story! *Heart emoji*

George Goode reply to Missy Clarke's comment: You should totally ask them, Mrs. C. Right to their face.

Rock Goode reply to Raymond 'Sheriff' Taylor's post: Please tell me this is just about the throwing up incident and nothing more sinister took place?

Raymond 'Sheriff' Taylor reply to Rock Goode's comment: Danny checked her out and she doesn't appear to have been violated

George Goode reply to Raymond 'Sheriff' Taylor's comment: Until Danny stuck his hand up there *laugh emoji*

Tansie Goode reply to Raymond 'Sheriff' Taylor's post: I've got footage of the incident Sheriff. Does this clear it up?

[VIDEO]

RAYMOND 'SHERIFF' TAYLOR REPLY TO TANSIE GOODE'S COMMENT: THAT DOES SEEM QUITE CONCLUSIVE. THANK YOU TANSIE

JESSE CARTWRIGHT REPLY TO TANSIE GOODE'S COMMENT: EXCELLENT CAMERA WORK. CAN I PLEASE HAVE THIS TO PUT ON YOUTUBE?

TANSIE GOODE REPLY TO JESSE CARTWRIGHT'S COMMENT: I'VE ALREADY DONE IT. [LINK]

ZACK

JESSE CARTWRIGHT: I CAN'T BELIEVE YOU THREW UP ALL OVER MABEL! *LAUGH EMOJI*

I stare, bleary-eyed, at the text from my brother. I rub a hand over my eyes in an attempt to dislodge some of the crust that's formed, but when I crack them open again it still feels like my eyelids are being weighted down by cement.

ME: WHO THE FUCK IS MABEL?

I try to think back to last night, but my head is pounding and I'm having trouble piecing together what exactly happened. I remember there being alcohol—that much is fact. And I remember being completely mortified about something. Did I spew on someone in my drunken state?

I let out a groan and sink back into the mattress as a

fresh wave of mortification hits me. *Why* did I get so drunk? Only one answer springs to mind and it leaves me with a queasy feeling in my chest. *Slater Goode.* I'd been having a nice day with Harriett and Livia, and then Slater showed up at the saloon and *bam!* There goes all my sense of reason.

My phone chimes and I check to see another text from my brother.

JESSE CARTWRIGHT: *THE HORSE*

The words stir a vague memory, and I groan again as the image of me stumbling from the saloon before nearly crashing into a horse and then throwing up all over its hindquarters floods into my brain. *Jesus Christ.* And Jesse already knows about it? That must mean the entire town knows. Which isn't all that surprising considering they treat gossiping like it's an Olympic sport.

ME: *HOW DO YOU KNOW WHAT THE DAMN HORSE IS CALLED? OR THAT I THREW UP ON IT*

JESSE CARTWRIGHT: *YOU REALLY NEED TO JOIN THE FB GROUP LITTLE BROTHER. THEN YOU WON'T ALWAYS BE SO OUT OF THE LOOP *WINK EMOJI**

I manage to maneuver myself into a sitting position and slowly crawl out of bed, my head still throbbing mercilessly. I gather some clothes and am just about to head across the hall for a shower when my phone chimes again.

JESSE CARTWRIGHT: *[LINK]*

Against my better judgment, I click the link and let out a loud groan of annoyance as I'm taken to a YouTube video of me hurling all over Mabel the horse.

Me: You've got to be kidding me. There's a fucking video and it's on YouTube already???

Jesse Cartwright: Hey you should be grateful for that video! Hank Latham wanted to string you up for 'traumatizing' Mabel. And half the town thought you tried to make it with her

Me: THEY THOUGHT WHAT??

Jesse Cartwright: Calm down. The video cleared that up, didn't it? Now they've moved on to speculating on whether you and Slater will be getting back together

I groan in frustration. *Jesus fucking Christ.*

Jesse Cartwright: Seriously, bro, get on the FB group

With a roll of my eyes, I toss my phone down and head into the bathroom to take my shower. I'm feeling marginally better by the time I get out, but not much, so I rummage through the bathroom drawers until I find some aspirin.

When I get back to my bedroom, I find several new texts on my phone. Except they're not from Jesse this time.

Slater Goode: Hey, just wanted to see how you were doing after last night. Hope you're not feeling too cruddy *smile emoji*

Slater Goode: Also I got Tansie to take the video down from YouTube. Sorry about that. Although it did apparently help clear your name in the big case against Hank Latham so that's something...

Slater Goode: I just realized you might not have my

number anymore. This is Slater in case you were wondering

Slater Goode: *Oh and if this isn't Zack, like if he's changed numbers and if this is some random person who now has his old number I'm really sorry for bothering you, just ignore all these texts*

By the time I get to the final text, I'm grinning despite myself. I *so* don't want to be reacting this way, but I can't help it. It's Slater—awkwardly charming and considerate as always. But then I remember, and that warm little glow that was starting to burn in my chest is snuffed out completely; because he wasn't *always* considerate. There was that one time when he was the complete opposite of that. And there was absolutely nothing charming about him then.

Deciding I don't want to be rude, I send a quick text back before switching my phone off and slipping it into my back pocket.

Me: *Feeling better, thanks.*

I need food, and as much as I don't particularly want to face the town after last night's debacle and all the gossiping that's been going around today, I know I need the kind of food I can only get at the saloon.

"Well, here's trouble," George says with a smirk when I walk in and take a seat at the bar.

I scowl at him. "Just get me something fried. Please."

He chuckles. "You want some wine with that?"

"God no," I say, almost moaning in pain at the thought of drinking alcohol right now.

"How about the Wagyu burger and a double side of our special crispy fries?" George suggests.

I nod eagerly. "Yes. Perfect."

Without me having to ask, he slides a glass of water across the bar to me, offering a casual wink. "Food'll be about half an hour."

Fortunately, the saloon's pretty quiet today, which isn't all that surprising considering it's a Wednesday afternoon so most of the locals would be at work. From memory, this place does a roaring weekday breakfast trade, and it's always pretty busy at night regardless of what day of the week it is.

By the time I'm done devouring the incredible burger, I'm feeling much better, and even the occasional teasing remarks from passing locals are no longer getting under my skin.

I'm about to settle my bill and head out when I see a familiar figure enter the saloon. Scrambling off my stool, I rush to the doorway and throw my arms around Lawson. "Oh my god, what the hell are you doing here?"

He beams down at me, chuckling softly. "Wow. Why don't I ever get that reaction at home?"

I pull back and hit him playfully in the arm. "I'm serious. What are you doing here?"

"You *told* me to come here."

My brows draw together in confusion. "I did?"

"Yeah. You did. You said it was an emergency and that the situation was dire and that you didn't think you'd last the week." He gives a casual shrug. "I figured I should come on the off chance you'd been kidnapped and needed someone to pay a ransom."

"Oh…" I cringe guiltily as the memory of the emergency calls I made to Lawson last night hit me. I had, of course, been referring to the situation with Slater. Because the second I saw him, instead of the hurt and anger and hatred I've been training myself to feel over the past twelve years, all I felt was want, and need, and desire. So yes, the situation is very desperate indeed. "Sorry…I may have been a little drunk last night."

Lawson chuckles. "Yeah, I assumed that. And then I knew for sure when I saw the video."

I throw my head back as a fresh wave of mortification hits me. "Oh my god, you saw the video?"

"Jesse thought I'd enjoy it," he says with a shrug.

"He's dead to me. I have no brother."

8

From the private Facebook group 'Finchley Locals Community Hangout'

Post by Daphne St. Clair: PSA - the boarding house is now at capacity, so anyone coming from out of town for the funeral on Friday will need to find alternate accommodations

Missy Clarke reply to Daphne St. Clair's post: I thought you had a room left? I was going to suggest it to Bill's folks to save me making up the bed in my craft room

Daphne St. Clair reply to Missy Clarke's comment: Sorry, Missy. They didn't make a reservation and a young man just came in needing a room

Livia Goode reply to Daphne St. Clair's comment: A young man, you say? Tell us more!

Daphne St. Clair reply to Livia Goode's comment: Not much to tell. He's friends with Zack Cartwright apparently

*Missy Clarke reply to Daphne St. Clair's comment: Oh no! Do you think they're together? I was so hoping Zack and Slater would work things out *sad emoji**
Livia Goode reply to Missy Clarke's comment: If they were together wouldn't he be staying at Gloria's with Zack?
Gloria Cartwright reply to Missy Clarke's comment: His name is Lawson Hale and he's Zack's best friend from Chicago. They're not together but I wouldn't get your hopes up about Zack and Slater, Missy. Zack's just getting out of a relationship and he's only here for a few days.
Alice Ackerman reply to Gloria Cartwright's comment: A few days is plenty of time for love to bloom! Hammond and I only knew each other for twelve hours before we were married back in the seventies.
Gloria Cartwright reply to Alice Ackerman's comment: Yes but you were divorced three years later when you found out he was running an illegal ferret-trafficking ring out of your basement. That's not a brilliant go-to example of true love, Alice.

Slater

I run my palm over the smooth surface of the wood I've just sanded, clearing away the sheet of dust that's collected. I decide it needs one more go over before I'll be happy with it, and am just about to start up again when I hear the door of the refitted barn I use as my workroom sliding open.

I glance up to see my uncle Rock standing in the doorway, looking dusty and grimy from a morning's work on his orchard. My barn, and the house I'm fixing up next to it, sit on property that used to be part of Rock's orchard, so it's not unusual for him to stop by in the middle of his day.

"No work in town today?" Rock asks.

I shake my head. "Web and I wrapped up a job yesterday."

He lets out a wry breath. "Are you two ever going to make this partnership thing official?"

I offer a soft smile. "Chance is drawing up the papers for us right now," I tell him. "It should all be done and dusted by next week."

Really, we should have gone into partnership ages ago; we've been working together on bigger jobs for years now, so it makes sense to merge our businesses and halve all the overhead expenses. We just haven't gotten around to actually making it happen yet.

"That's great," Rock says with a nod, before gesturing to the project I'm currently working on, asking, "Something for the house?"

I shake my head. "It's for Nanna. I promised her a new porch swing ages ago but I never got around to it…"

Rock's face clouds with emotion, reminding me of the fact that I may have just lost my grandfather, but he's lost his dad. Swallowing hard, he asks, "You want some help with it?"

I shake my head. "Thanks, but I want to do this one on my own."

He nods in understanding and turns to leave. "I'll leave you to it, then. See you tomorrow, kid."

Once he's gone, I get back to work on the swing. While I love carpentry and the domestic building work I do for my business, to me that's work. Whereas furniture making is a hobby—something I find completely relaxing. I've been asked many times if I love it so much why didn't I just become a joiner like Web? But the answer is simple: because I didn't want to.

I didn't want the joy I get from creating something to be stripped away by having to work to someone else's needs and specifications. Everything I make is purely because I want to.

It sounds totally clichéd to say it, but when I come here to my workroom I'm filled with a sense of peace. Today's the first time I've felt anything like it since getting the news on Sunday.

Later in the day, I stop by Web's place to say hi to his brother, Kip, who's just flown in from Alabama. On a private jet, no less.

Kip's the only one of us Goode's who has left Finchley permanently, although I guess you can't blame the guy considering he's shacked up with one of the richest men in the country. Not that that's why he fell for Preston, obviously. Actually, now that I think about it, none of us really know how the two of them fell for each other. It all happened far away from town and outside the sphere of the Finchley gossip mill.

"Hey, nice to meet you," Preston says, taking my hand

in a firm grip and offering a winning smile that I'm sure must be used to win negotiations on a regular basis. "Wish it were under better circumstances."

I nod, offering a polite smile. "Same here."

After releasing my hand, Preston returns to sit on the sofa next to Kip, snuggling up nice and close in a way that makes Web clear his throat on the other side of the living room. I glance over to find him standing there with his arms folded over his chest, his eyes fixed on his brother rather pointedly.

"Do you need a lozenge?" Kip asks, one eyebrow raised.

"I'm good," Web says gruffly.

I know when Kip first told us about Preston, Web had a difficult time coming around to the idea. Partly because it meant his brother would be moving away permanently, and partly because he just couldn't get his mind around the rather significant age difference—Preston is in his mid-forties, at least seventeen years older than Kip. But over time, Web seemed to come around; and I guess the fact that Kip seemed so happy kind of made it impossible for Web to continue mounting protests. But clearly he's still a little on the fence about becoming a fully paid up member of the We Heart Preston Club if his body language now is anything to go by.

"So, how long are you guys staying?" I ask, mainly to break the silence that's been drawing out.

"Just for the weekend," Kip says. "Preston needs to get back for a big client meeting on Monday."

Web mutters something under his breath that sounds a bit like *Of course he does*, and I shoot him a look telling him to cut it out. If he's not careful he'll end up ruining the few days Kip is in town.

After about another half hour of excruciating small talk between me, Kip, and Preston—and intermittent grunts from Web—Kip and Preston decide to make their exit, evidently heading to the saloon to meet up with Tansie and some of the rest of the family.

Once they're gone, Web tosses his head back, letting out a heavy sigh.

"You need to make more of an effort with him," I say sternly.

He lifts his gaze to meet mine, eyes wide with incredulity. "You've got to be kidding me."

I shake my head. "Not even remotely." Letting out a soft sigh, I pin him with an intent look, saying, "Web, Kip's nuts about this guy. He's not going anywhere. So, what are you going to do? Just grunt at him while he tries to make awkward conversation for the rest of your life?"

Web rakes a frustrated hand through his tangle of dark waves. "It's just… He's not—"

"Who you pictured your brother to end up with?" I supply. "Yeah, no shit. But that doesn't mean they're not right for each other. And just think about it—how would you feel if his family treated Kip this way?"

That seems to get through to him and he lets his eyes fall closed, releasing a defeated sigh. "You're right."

"Of course I am," I say simply, offering a wry smirk.

"Fine, so what am I supposed to do now?"

I shrug. "I don't know. Maybe you could start by joining them at the saloon tonight. Talk to the guy. Get to know him a little."

He nods. "Okay. Yeah, I guess I can do that. You want to come with?"

I shake my head. "Nah, this is your thing, man."

Not to mention, if I eat at the saloon yet again this week I'll have trouble fitting into my pants.

9

From the private Facebook group 'Finchley Locals Community Hangout'

Post by Candace Goode: Attention all: tomorrow's service will begin at 12.30 sharp, as Reverend Lockwood has double-booked and needs to be in Placer for a wedding at 2pm. A wake will follow at Walker and Genevieve's, where we'll be serving burgers, ribs, and many, many, MANY different varieties of bean casserole generously donated by the lovely locals. George, Tansie, and Rock will be in charge of refreshments so driving is not recommended.

Hank Latham reply to Candace Goode's post: I gave that casserole to your grandmother to help her through her hour of need

Candace Goode reply to Hank Latham's comment: And she very much appreciates it

Gunner Clarke reply to Candace Goode's post: How many different types of bean casserole are there?

Candace Goode reply to Gunner Clarke's comment: Oh, you'll find out tomorrow *wink emoji*

Zack

On Thursday night, the day before the funeral, Jesse arrives in Finchley. He gets in at around six pm, and it's not long before the suggestion is made to head out to eat. And seeing as how we're in Finchley, there's really only one place to go…

"Have I mentioned how awesome I think this place is?" Lawson says as we slide into a booth at the saloon. There's a wide grin on his face as he glances around at his surroundings.

"You just like it because you think 'saloon' is a funny word," I point out.

Lawson shrugs. "Well, you've got me there."

We give our drinks order to the server and take a few minutes to look over the menu.

"*Damn*, who is *that?*" Lawson asks, practically drooling as his eyes follow someone across the other side of the saloon.

Curious, I turn to see who's captured his attention and see Web has just entered the saloon and is making his way toward the bar where a small cluster of Goodes are gathered, along with Gunner Clarke and an attractive older guy I think must be Kip Goode's boyfriend, based on the way his hand seems glued to the younger man's ass. I feel a weird pinching sensation in my gut when I realize Slater's not with Web; it's relief, obviously. Definitely relief.

"That's Web," I tell Lawson.

His brows shoot up. "Web? That's a name?"

"It's short for Webster."

"Like the dictionary?"

I chuckle. "Yeah, like the dictionary."

Lawson lets out a small breath of laughter, shaking his head in amusement before returning his gaze to Web, who, I have to admit, is looking pretty good these days. He's got a scruffy, lumbersexual look going on that's really working for him, even if I personally prefer a guy who's clean-shaven.

"He's hot," Lawson says appreciatively, finally turning his attention back to us.

Jesse casts a narrowed glance in the direction of the bar before releasing a disgruntled huff. "Please, I've seen better looking slugs," he says with no small dose of disdain dripping from his voice.

Lawson's brows shoot up in surprise. "You know, Jess, I just don't think that's true."

I shake my head in exasperation as I watch Jesse scowl into his scotch and soda. Jesse and Web are the same age, and growing up they were always the best of friends. Practically inseparable. I have no idea what happened to cause it, but at some point during high school everything changed. Now even the merest mention of Webster Goode is enough to darken Jesse's mood.

"How's David?" I ask, hoping the change of subject will liven Jesse up.

It does.

"He's great," Jesse says, smiling brightly. "He wanted to come this weekend, but he has to work."

With great effort, I manage not to groan. Or roll my eyes. Or glance at Lawson to see his reaction…

David *always* has to work. And if it's not work, it's a trip he can't possibly get out of. Or an important engagement that he's only just remembered he has. Or a sudden aversion to the food served at the restaurant I've booked after Jesse assured me it's one of David's favorites.

They've been together three years and I've met the guy twice. Both times were when I was visiting New York. Both times were at their apartment. Once was when I showed up fifteen minutes early to pick Jesse up and David was rushing out the door mumbling something about a sick aunt, and the other was when we hit a bar after dinner one time and saw his 'important work function' was code for pounding shots with his friends.

Needless to say, I'm not a fan of the guy. But Jesse loves him and if he makes my brother happy I guess that's all that matters. Besides, who am I to judge, really? It was only two weeks ago that I caught the man I'd thought was *so* perfect screwing a nineteen-year-old named Piedro.

❅

IT'S A CLICHÉD STATEMENT, I know, but Ted's funeral service is lovely. Each of his four sons speak, telling stories that are equal parts sweet, sad, and hilarious. As I listen to them, I'm filled with that same sense of regret that I didn't get back to visit more often since moving away, but I guess there's no point in dwelling on that now.

After the service, it feels like the entire town heads back to Walker and Genevieve's—Slater's parents—place for a rather rowdy wake featuring hamburgers, ribs, and way too much alcohol.

"Jesus, when did Tucker Goode become a giant?" I mutter, watching in awe as the youngest of our generation of Goodes crosses the backyard to join a conversation between his sister Everley and a girl I don't recognize.

Jesse chuckles beside me. "When was the last time you saw him?"

"I don't know. Clearly not for a while." Tucker used to be a miniature version of Slater; now he'd be at least several inches taller than his brother. And Slater's already over six feet himself.

"Is every member of this family descended from Greek gods?" Lawson asks, gazing at Tucker with unmistakable interest.

"Don't even think about it," I warn. "He's only twenty." I don't add the part about Tucker being straight; that'd only interest Lawson further.

Law gives a lazy one-shouldered shrug. "It's legal."

"Slater would kill you," I tell him.

Lawson chuckles. "You'd avenge me, wouldn't you?"

Grinning, Jesse says, "I'd be more worried about Ax. He's the hot-head of the family."

"Which one's he again?" Lawson asks.

"Slater's older brother," I say, pointing Axel out and

rolling my eyes as Law whistles through his teeth. "Can you try *not* springing a boner right now? We're at a wake."

"Z, the guy died having sex. I'm sure he wouldn't mind."

"Alright, Zack, Lawson, you two need to do shots!" George commands, appearing seemingly out of nowhere holding up two shot glasses, both filled with clear liquid.

Lawson takes one without question, but I'm more hesitant. "Why, exactly, do we need to do this?"

"Those are the rules," George explains. "Anyone who mentions sex, or anything related to it has to drink a shot."

I screw my face up in confusion. "What? That's crazy. How are you possibly going to police that?"

George offers a wicked grin. "We have spies in every conversation, man."

With a roll of my eyes, I take the shot from his hand. Across the room, I see Slater and Chance are suffering the same treatment, with Tansie watching over them like a hawk as they down their shots. *Damn, he looks good in that suit...* the thought spurs me out of my hesitation and I lift the shot to my lips, wincing at the taste of the tequila. Of course, it *had* to be tequila...

"Nice job," George says with a nod, as though Lawson and I have achieved something spectacular by swallowing an ounce and a half of tequila. "But can I just express how disappointed and hurt I am that it was *Axel* who gave you that boner?" he says, eyeing Lawson with big, mournful eyes. "I mean, look at *that*. And then look at *this*..." He gestures lazily to Axel before gliding his hand in a seductive motion down the side of his leanly muscled frame and then over what I can objectively admit is a pretty nice ass. His expression turns playful as he says, "Are you telling me you wouldn't rather get with *this?*"

Jesse and I are both shaking with laughter as, for once in his life, Lawson seems at a complete loss for what to say.

"By your own rules you have to take a shot now," I say to George. "I mean, I'm assuming talking about boners and rubbing your own ass counts as being sex-related?"

George chuckles, grinning broadly. "Good point. But at least I get to take you down with me."

I groan as I realize my fatal mistake, while George lifts a hand to get Tansie's attention and calls for two shots.

This is going to be a *long* day.

10

From the private Facebook group 'Finchley Locals Community Hangout'

Post by Missy Clarke: *eggplant emoji* *eggplant emoji* *eggplant emoji*

Gunner Clarke reply to Missy Clarke's post: Mom! Stop! What are you doing???

Missy Clarke reply to Gunner Clarke's comment: What? I like eggplants

Kip Goode reply to Missy Clarke's comment: Me too, Mrs. C *wink emoji*

Gunner Clarke reply to Missy Clarke's comment: *face palm emoji*

"Ooh, honey, you need to do a shot!" my mom cries.

My brow furrows in confusion. I'd been chatting to Beth Bowry about one of her recipes; there had definitely been no mention whatsoever of sex. "What are you talking about?"

"You said the 'E' word," Mom says, as though she's a detective who's caught me in an elaborate lie.

"Eggplant?" I ask, still confused. "Mom, Beth and I were talking about her eggplant lasagna recipe."

Mom shakes her head. "I wasn't born yesterday, Slater. I know what that emoji means."

Next to her, Missy Clarke is wearing an entirely characteristic look of confusion on her face. "What does it mean?"

"It means 'cock', Missy," Mom explains. "It's what you use when you're texting to represent a penis."

I bring a hand up to cover my face. "Jesus Christ, I don't even want to know how you know that."

"From when your father and I sext, of course," Mom says, clearly not registering the part about me *not wanting to know*.

A look of dawning comprehension crosses Missy's face. "Well, that...explains some things. Why an eggplant, though? I would have thought a zucchini would be more accurate..."

Okay, I need to eject myself from this conversation *right now*. I excuse myself and head into the house to use the bathroom. Finding the downstairs one occupied, I head upstairs instead.

I'm just about to knock on the door when it swings open and I find myself face-to-face with Zack. I stare at him for a long moment, and he stares back, the air between us growing more and more charged as neither of us seems to be able to look away.

Eventually, he moves. But it's not to brush past me. It's to reach out, grab my tie, and tug me into the bathroom, slamming the door behind me and pressing me up against it.

His lips on mine are achingly familiar, and despite my surprise I respond instantly. I wrap my arms around his waist, tugging him closer and bending my head down farther so I can deepen the kiss. It's intense, and intoxicating. And so, so perfect.

Finally, Zack tears his lips from mine, breathing heavily as he stares up at me with wide eyes, as though he can't quite believe what just happened. "I shouldn't have done that."

I arch an eyebrow at him. "Why did you?"

He hesitates for a moment, dragging his teeth over his bottom lip in a way that almost makes me groan out loud. "Tequila makes me do dumb things."

I let out a soft chuckle. "Yeah? Like what?"

"Like…TPing my boss's office and getting myself fired…"

My brows shoot up in surprise. That is *so* not something I'd ever picture Zack doing. "Did he deserve it at least?"

Zack shrugs. "Well, I walked in on him screwing his nineteen-year-old intern, so…"

I wince. "Yeah, not a great boss."

"And we were dating at the time, so not a great boyfriend either."

I don't let it show on my face, but I'm secretly planning to track this asshole down and cause him immense physical pain for hurting Zack like that. But right now I simply offer Zack an impressed smile. "Well, in that case, I think TPing his office was a very *smart* move. Just like kissing me."

Zack rolls his eyes, but I don't give him a chance to respond as I crash my lips back against his in a needy, desperate kiss. He doesn't hesitate or try to pull away, instead sinking into the kiss and allowing me to spin us around so he's the one pinned against the wall.

I shove my thigh between his legs, groaning softly against his lips as I feel his hard cock rubbing against me.

"Tell me," I murmur as I move my kisses to Zack's neck, loving the way he practically purrs as one of my hands slides into the back of his pants.

"What?" he asks, almost panting.

I slide my fingers over his crease before running them slowly around his ring. "Tell me the truth," I clarify as I continue to tease him. "Why did you really kiss me?"

Zack's head falls back against the closed bathroom door and he lets out a shaky breath, his eyes screwing shut as he pants, "Fuck, Jesus, fuck…"

With a soft chuckle, I withdraw my hand from his pants and spit on my fingers. Then I return them to Zack's ass, pushing inside his hole and damn near exploding from the combination of having part of my body inside his tight heat, and the rumbling groan of pleasure he lets out as I breach him.

His fingers dig into my shoulders, his hips jutting madly into my thigh as I continue to finger his ass.

"Tell me, Zack," I command.

"Because I fucking wanted to!" He finally admits on a gasped breath.

My mouth curves into a satisfied grin and I lean in to press a kiss to the underside of his jaw. "That wasn't so hard to admit, was it?"

"I seriously hate you," he growls, before letting out another strangled groan as I twist my hand a little.

"Tell me the rest, baby," I murmur. "You know what I want to hear."

"Slater…"

I lift my focus to his face, staring deep into his eyes and practically forcing him to answer with the intensity of my gaze.

"I've wanted it for days," he whispers. "Since I saw you on Tuesday."

I crash my lips against his, my unspoken 'me too' clear as day in the kiss.

We finally break apart, and I breathe out a soft chuckle at the little whimper Zack lets out as I pull my fingers from his ass. "What else do you want?"

He glares at me, eyes full of heat and anticipation. "You know what I want."

My mouth curves into a grin of approval and I take a small step back. "Come on. Not here." I grab Zack's wrist and open the bathroom door, leading him across the hall to my old bedroom.

As soon as we're inside with the door closed, we start attacking each other, ripping off layers of clothing while attempting to grab as much of each other's skin as possible.

Once we're both completely naked, I push Zack onto the bed and crawl up on top of him.

"Are you on PrEP?"

He nods emphatically. "And I got tested recently."

I offer a soft quirk of my lips before leaning down to drop a soft kiss to his cheek. "Perfect."

I slide off him and wander over to the nightstand to where I know there's a bottle of lube somewhere in the drawer. I don't actually live in this house anymore, but I crash here often, and, well…a guy needs his supplies.

Finally wrapping my hands around the bottle, I toss it to Zack, who catches it deftly. "Get yourself ready, babe," I tell him. "I want to watch."

His eyes flare with anticipation and he offers a brief smile before moving into a better position for fingering himself. I let out a soft groan at the sight of his cock tapping against his abs. Hard and pulsing…for *me*. I'm tempted to just dive on him and take that gorgeous dick in my mouth, to suck him hard and deep until he comes in a rush down my throat…

But I manage to control the urge. We'll have time for that later. Right now I need to keep hands and mouth and everything else off and just watch.

The breathy moans of pleasure Zack lets out as he fucks himself with his fingers are the sexiest sounds I've ever heard, and the way he's writhing on the bed, looking thoroughly debauched, has me so turned on I can barely restrain myself from stepping forward and replacing his fingers with my own. Or my tongue. Or my dick.

Finally, after what seems like an eternity, Zack withdraws his fingers and gets to his knees, shuffling across the mattress until he's right at the edge, facing me. He reaches out to slide his hands over my biceps, flashing me a heated look. "I'm ready…"

"Thank fucking god," I say with a groan, before grabbing Zack around the waist and tossing him back on the bed. It takes me a mere moment to throw his legs over my shoulders and sink deep inside him.

"Fuck, fuck, fuck, Slate…" Zack groans as I fill him.

I give him a brief moment to adjust before I feel his hands on my ass, spurring me to move. I don't hesitate to respond, snapping my hips in a steady tempo of hard, deep thrusts.

I'm finding it a little hard to believe where I am right now, if I'm being honest. Despite my best efforts over the years, I've dreamed of this moment countless times. The moment I'd get to have Zack Cartwright in my arms again, kiss him again, be inside him again… I know it's not healthy, spending twelve years hung up on a person who moved on a long time ago, but there's just something about Zack I've never been able to shake. Even if all I have is tonight, I plan to make the most of every single moment.

And, Jesus, he just looks so fucking perfect spread out in front of me like this, his dark waves flying all over the place as his head thrashes about with the intensity of his pleasure. The pleasure *I'm* bringing him.

I lean down closer, practically folding his body in half between us. He lets out a strangled groan as the movement lets me push even deeper inside him, but it's cut short as I slam my mouth to his.

His hands fly into my hair, tugging at the strands in a way that's so familiar it makes me almost want to cry.

I tear my mouth from his and let out a groan, feeling the climax building inside me. "Fuck, I'm going to come..."

Zack nods eagerly. "God, yeah," he pants. "Fill my ass, Slate."

I slam my lips back to his, increasing my tempo as I chase the orgasm. It doesn't take long before I'm groaning into his mouth, my grip on his flesh tightening as I completely explode.

I take a few moments to get my breath back before untangling Zack's legs from my shoulders and setting his feet back on the mattress. Pulling out of him, I sink to my knees beside the bed and lean over so I can *finally* get a taste of that beautiful cock.

"Jesus...*fuck...*" Zack groans as I wrap my mouth around him, swirling my tongue over his cockhead before taking him farther down. His hands fly into my hair, tugging hard in that way I absolutely love, as his hips jut off the bed, pushing his cock deeper into my mouth.

And I love it. I love how crazy I'm driving him right now. And I love how familiar it all is. It only takes a few minutes of me swallowing his cock before he's arching off the bed and coming in a rush down my throat.

"Sorry," he says, still struggling for breath as I pull off his dick after lapping up every drop of cum. "I should have—that was just—"

I grin at him. "The first of many orgasms you'll be having tonight."

"Uh huh," Zack says, looking so blissed out I'm not sure he even knows what he's agreed to.

I chuckle and stand so I can lean over the bed and press a soft kiss to his lips. "Wait here for a minute."

"I can't even feel my legs right now—where am I going to go?"

Grinning, I quickly shove my legs into my suit pants and fling on my shirt. I don't bother with doing all the buttons up or tucking it in. Everyone downstairs is so wasted right now I can't imagine they'll even notice my disheveled appearance. Besides, I'll only be down there for a minute or so. "I'll be back in a sec," I tell Zack, before leaving the bedroom and creeping downstairs.

As predicted, everyone at the wake is so hammered thanks to George and Tansie's shots, I'm practically invisible as I move quickly into the kitchen to grab a large bottle of water and a few packets of chips from my mom's pantry, as well as a pack of baby wipes she keeps handy for when Ethan gets all messy—which is a lot.

It's not until I have my bare foot on the bottom step, ready to head back upstairs that I'm stopped by someone…

"Hey, have you seen my brother?"

I spin around to find Jesse standing there with a concerned frown on his face. As he rakes his eyes over me, however, the frown reforms into a knowing smirk and he gives a small shrug. "Never mind."

Not wanting to linger any further, I spin back around and rush up the stairs. When I enter the bedroom, I find Zack in the exact same position I left him in: spread out on the bed, legs dangling over the edge of the mattress.

The sight brings a little life back to my cock and I know it's not going to be long before I'm ready to go again.

I stalk over to the bed and toss my haul down. "I brought supplies. To help you refresh and recharge."

Zack blinks up at me in what appears to be part confusion, part disappointment. "Why do you have clothes on?"

I arch an eyebrow at him, my mouth curving in an amused smirk. "I thought people would probably take more notice of me if I went downstairs stark naked."

Zack nods and slowly starts getting up. Once he's on his knees, he shuffles across the mattress until he's right in front of me. "I guess that makes sense. But you don't need them on *now*." He reaches up to unfasten the two buttons I'd hastily done up, before slipping my shirt from my shoulders. Then he moves to my pants, leaving me completely naked again.

He reaches for my half-hard cock and I hiss through my teeth as he starts gently stroking it. That merges into a full-on groan as he reaches around to tease my hole.

"Get on the bed, Slater," he commands. "I want to taste this ass."

I'm practically numb with anticipation, and it's all I can do to flop down onto the bed, my ass in the air presented to Zack like an offering. One that he accepts eagerly and with great enthusiasm.

The way he works me with his talented mouth drives me so fucking crazy, it's not long before I find myself hurtling over the edge for the second time tonight. I thought the earlier orgasm was incredible, but this is even better, and afterward all I can manage to do is collapse onto the bed, right on top of the wet spot I've just made.

All I can think is thank god I had the foresight to gather those supplies, because I'll really be needing some sustenance after this.

※

We manage to get a couple hours' sleep in between all the sex and the joking around and the eating potato chips off each other's chests—which is actually sexier than it sounds, although still kind of messy. But by the time morning comes around, I can tell Zack is in two minds over all this. One mind is the one controlled by his cock, and it's telling him to proceed full speed ahead; the other is his more logical brain—the one that has to think every decision through and analyze it from every angle—and that one's starting to kick in and tell him this isn't such a great idea.

Personally, I'm not even remotely conflicted right now. I love him. I've loved him since we were fourteen years old, and I never stopped; even when I know I probably should have. But that's not what he feels. To him this is…well, I'm not entirely sure what. Nostalgia, maybe? Chemistry?

Whatever it is, I'll take it…

11

From the private Facebook group 'Finchley Locals Community Hangout'

Post by Genevieve Goode: Thank you everyone who came yesterday to help us celebrate Ted's life. It was a great day, all things considered, I'm sure Ted would have loved it!

Hank Latham reply to Genevieve Goode's post: Genevieve, your son is the devil

Genevieve Goode reply to Hank Latham's comment: Which one?

Hank Latham reply to Genevieve Goode's comment: George. He kept forcing tequila down my throat yesterday

Genevieve Goode reply to Hank Latham's comment: George isn't my son Hank

Hank Latham reply to Genevieve Goode's comment: Well then who's son is he?

Candace Goode reply to Hank Latham's comment: No

ONE REALLY KNOWS. HE JUST SHOWED UP ONE DAY LIKE A KID FROM A HORROR MOVIE…
LORELAI GOODE REPLY TO HANK LATHAM'S COMMENT: DON'T TALK ABOUT MY BABY LIKE THAT!

ZACK

MY CONVERSATION with Slater plays in my head over and over as I make my way from his parents' place to my mom's.

"…it was a one-night only deal. Call it a bonus night or whatever. It's over now. We're done."

"If you say so."

I shake my head, furious at myself. I can't believe I let him kiss me after that. One brush of his lips and it took all the willpower I possessed not to just fall into bed with him all over again…so much for my defiant declaration.

Argh, this is bad. So, so bad. I mean, it was good—really, really, *really* good. But that in itself is bad. Because I just can't want Slater. And at least before we hooked up I could tell myself the sex would be terrible. Now, I have concrete proof that it's anything but.

Fucking hell, I'm such a mess.

When I arrive home, it's to find my mom sitting at the kitchen table eating a bowl of oatmeal. She's dressed in her nursing scrubs, and I vaguely recall her leaving the wake early last night so she could get to work.

She looks up as I enter the kitchen, her eyebrow

arched as she glances over my disheveled appearance. "Do I want to know?"

I let out a wry breath. "I'm sure you can probably guess."

She offers me a considering look before returning to her oatmeal. "Is it...serious?"

I shake my head adamantly. "One-time thing. Just a backslide."

She nods. "Okay."

Like I said, Mom and I don't really do the close communication stuff. This is pretty much as deep as our conversations go. With a shrug, I grab a bottle of water from the fridge and head up to my room, where I strip out of what's left of my suit and slide under the covers of my bed.

"Why the fuck are you calling me at five am?" Lawson demands after answering his phone on my third attempt at calling.

"I slept with Slater," I blurt out. "Like, a lot. I don't know how many times. I lost track. But it was a lot. Like, *so* many times. My ass is killing me right now."

"Uhh...how, exactly..." Lawson says, clearly struggling for words. "I mean...what happened?"

"I don't know," I moan in frustration. "One minute you and I were talking to Everley about *Real Vegas Weddings,* and the next I was in the bathroom and Slater and I were making out and he put his finger up my ass and things just kind of went from there..."

"Well, I'm not exactly surprised you two hooked up. But, seriously...at a wake?"

I let out an annoyed groan. "Because I needed to feel worse about this. Thanks."

Lawson chuckles softly. "Why do you feel bad? Sounds like you should be over the moon right now. I definitely would be after a night like that."

"Because it's Slater!" I whisper-yell, not wanting to wake Jesse in the room next door. "I can't hook up with Slater, Law. I can't go down that road…"

"Well, I hate to point out the obvious, Z, but you've already gone down it."

"I seriously hate you," I mutter.

Lawson just lets out a low chuckle.

There's a beat of silence before I move the topic on to something else that's been on my mind. "Hey, Law?"

"Mmhmm?"

"Don't go after George."

He's quiet for a long moment before saying, "What?"

"I know he messes around a lot," I say carefully, "but he's completely straight."

Lawson lets out a heavy sigh. "I know that, Z. I'm not an idiot."

"Okay…just making sure."

LATER IN THE DAY, once I've had a few hours' sleep, I decide to venture out into town. I bump into Harriett and her younger sister Delia in Main Street, and we're trying to decide what to do for lunch when a commotion erupts nearby.

Turning around, I see Mrs. Ackerman and Hank

Latham involved in a heated argument that's drawn the attention of several passersby.

"I've told you before, Hank, we can't be talking like this—if you have issues with the way this is being handled you need to take it up with my lawyer."

"Your lawyer is my lawyer, Alice! He's the only one in town!"

"Then you shouldn't have any problem talking to him," Mrs. Ackerman replies testily.

"You're being completely unreasonable," Hank growls.

"*I'm* being unreasonable? This whole situation is your fault!"

"*My* fault? It happened on *your* property."

"And you should be thankful I'm not pursuing trespassing charges!"

I finally manage to tear my eyes away from the argument, glancing at Delia and Harriett in utter confusion. "What the hell's going on?"

"Custody battle," Delia explains. "It's getting pretty heated. Really stressing Chance out."

My eyes widen in shock. *"What?* Hank and Mrs. Ackerman? *Custody?"* Mrs. Ackerman is in her mid-seventies, at least, and Hank would have to be a good ten years older. As far as I know there's no romantic history whatsoever between them…

"Puppy custody," Harriett clarifies. "Apparently Hank's dog, Butch, got out a few weeks ago and snuck into Mrs. A's yard while Fifi was in heat. Now she's pregnant and they're fighting over the puppies."

Wow. I can definitely understand Mrs. Ackerman's anger now. Fifi is a prized purebred show poodle; this pregnancy is likely to force her into retirement. Hank's probably lucky he's not being sued.

"How many puppies are they expecting?" I ask.

"Four, I think," Harriett says.

"Can't they just take two each?"

Delia shrugs. "You'd think so, but Mrs. A doesn't want to separate Fifi from her babies, and Hank thinks any pups of Butch's will need a lot of space to run around, so he wants them on his farm."

"And Chance is stuck in the middle?" I venture, remembering what the arguing pair had said about him being the only lawyer in town.

Both Harriett and Delia nod.

"Yep," Harriet says, offering a wry smile. "But at least he's getting paid twice over."

I shake my head with amusement. Seriously, this town...

"Okay, so lunch," Delia says, getting us back on topic. "How about Jones's?"

"Oh, yeah, sounds good," Harriett agrees.

"What's Jones's?" I ask.

"It's that little restaurant where the medical practice used to be," Harriett explains. "The food's amazing."

My eyes light up immediately and I can already feel my stomach growling. "Oh, yeah, that place looks great."

Before we can get on our way, we're intercepted by Missy Clarke. "Oh, girls, I'm so glad I ran into you. Yesterday was lovely. I think Ted would have really enjoyed it."

"Thanks, Mrs. Clarke," Harriett says, smiling brightly.

"And you," Missy says, turning her attention to me, her

eyes twinkling with excitement. "A birdie told me you spent the night at the Goodes? I do hope this means you and Slater are getting back together—I've been rooting for you two for years!"

My eyes widen as I'm taken aback by her enthusiasm. "Uh…I'm not…I mean, we don't…"

"Hey, Mrs. Clarke," Delia jumps in, saving me from my floundering, "would you like to join us for lunch? We were thinking of going to Jones's—they serve a really nice eggplant parmesan."

"Oh, I do like eggplant," Missy says wistfully, and having joined the town Facebook group this morning I'm having a hard time keeping a straight face, right along with Delia and Harriett. "But I have a hair appointment in half an hour, so I'll have to miss this time. Rain check?"

Harriett nods. "Absolutely."

"That was a little risky," I comment once Missy's bustled off. It was amusing, but I'm not sure I'd be able to handle and entire lunch with Missy Clarke.

Delia waves my comment away. "She gets her hair done at one pm every Sunday. It was low risk."

"So, shall we?" Harriett suggests.

I'm about to agree when my attention is caught by something—someone, to be more specific—across the other side of the street. Slater has just emerged from the saloon and, as though sensing my presence, he glances up, his eyes immediately finding mine. He offers a soft quirk of his lips and begins crossing the street.

"Oh oh, I think we've lost Zack," I hear Harriett say wryly from what seems like very far away.

"Hey," Slater says once he's standing right in front of

me. Then, as if only just noticing they're there, he turns to his cousins and offers a soft smile, "Hey, Deels. Hey, Harri."

"Hey, Slater," they both say, their faces split into matching grins. I've never thought these two looked all that much alike, but right now they seem almost as identical as Harriett and Livia.

"Do you want us to give you a minute?" Harriett asks.

"No," I say.

And at the same time, Slater says, "Yes."

Both Harriett and Delia chuckle. Delia turns to me, offering a sly smile. "We'll save you a seat at the restaurant. But don't worry if you lose track of time and don't manage to join us." And with a parting wink, she and Harriett turn on their heels and saunter off up Main Street, leaving me to my fate.

12

From the private Facebook group 'Finchley Locals Community Hangout'

Post by Beth Bowry: Does anyone have a good hangover remedy?

George Goode reply to Beth Bowry's post: Hair of the dog *wink emoji*

Missy Clarke reply to George Goode's comment: Beth do not do this! Dog hair should not be ingested by humans!

Gunner Clarke reply to Missy Clarke's comment: Mom that's not what 'hair of the dog' means *face palm emoji*

Missy Clarke reply to Gunner Clarke's comment: It's not?

"I'm sure this will do a lot to stop the gossip," Zack says dryly as I grasp his elbow, guiding him away from the center of town to somewhere more private.

I let out a soft chuckle. "Don't worry. I'll just ask Candace to have another baby. That'll get them talking about something else."

Amusement lights Zack's eyes and his lips spread into a wry smile. "Yeah, I'm sure with three kids already she'd be thrilled to do us that favor."

"Here…" I direct us toward the blacksmith's, which has been preserved by the county's historical society and is one of the town's main tourist attractions. It's closed at the moment, though, so I usher Zack around the side to where a wooden partition will block us from the view of passersby on the street.

I press him back against the partition and take a step closer so we're flush together, my hands coming up to gently squeeze his sides. I draw in a breath of anticipation before lowering my head…but before I can reach his lips, he slaps his palm to my mouth, holding me back.

"No. Wait…"

I hesitate for a moment before gently prying his hand away from my mouth, taking the opportunity to thread my fingers through his. "What is it?"

There's a stubborn jut to his jaw as he eyes me intently. "I meant what I said this morning. We can't do this again."

I glance down between us to where our groins are practically molded together, before lifting my gaze back to Zack's, one eyebrow raised. His cheeks flush adorably pink at my unspoken observation, and I watch as he swallows deeply, my cock pulsing at the sight of his bobbing throat.

"It's not a good idea," Zack murmurs in what I'm sure he intends to be a firm voice, but it comes out a little ragged.

The corner of my mouth quirks up and I shake my head slowly. "Oh, baby. We both know it's a *very* good idea."

"I'm only here until Thursday," he points out. "Not even a week."

I lift my free hand to graze his lightly stubbled jaw. "So we make it a temporary thing. Like a…vacation fling," I suggest. The words feel wrong in my mouth. There's nothing temporary about what I want with Zack, but I know there's no chance he'll go for anything more right now.

He offers me a considering look, his plump bottom lip jutting out in the kind of way that makes it impossible for me to stop myself from gently running my thumb over it. His stormy gray eyes meet mine for a long moment before his tongue sneaks out of his mouth to lazily lap at my thumb.

I let out a soft groan before snatching my hand away from his mouth and crashing my lips against his. The wooden partition rattles as I shove Zack harder against it, pinning him tight with my body.

"Just this week," he gasps in between frantic kisses, his hands tugging so desperately at my hair I'll no doubt look like I've been electrocuted once we're done. "Just until I go home," he clarifies. "Just sex."

I don't answer audibly, instead giving what I'm sure passes as a nod as I claim his lips again, my hands roaming over his body until I reach the waistband of his jeans. He's only giving me half of what I really want—if I had my way he wouldn't even be talking about going home—but I have a few days to convince him this is where he should be. That *I'm* who he should be with…

But right now, I just desperately need to get my mouth on this gorgeous cock.

"Oh, look, Bob—there *are* people there! I told you it would be open by now."

"But the sign says closed, love. We should come back—"

"Don't be silly! They're right here—we'll just ask them…"

Zack and I have completely frozen, and are staring at each other, silent and wide-eyed, as it occurs to us the man and woman—who must be tourists, based off their British accents—are talking about the blacksmith's. And us.

After exchanging a helpless glance, Zack and I pry ourselves away from each other. I take a moment to straighten myself up before stepping out from around the partition.

"Hello, there," I say, waving at the couple, who appear to be around sixty or so.

The woman beams at me, while the man looks away awkwardly; I have the impression he's not quite as oblivious as his wife in regards to what I was doing behind the partition just now. "Oh, hello!" she says brightly. "Can you help us out? We'd like to have a look inside. Your website says this is a must-see place in town."

"Well, that's true," I say, giving a polite nod. "But unfortunately, as you can see, it's not open right now. The blacksmith's is only open to the public until midday each day."

The woman's face crumples. "Couldn't you make an exception? Today's our last day in town."

I cringe at her words, knowing there's no way I could let them into the site without breaking a window or something. And Tansie would kill me if I attempted that. I shake my head apologetically, deciding to just go with the truth. "I'm sorry, ma'am. It's actually my sister who runs this site, and she's off giving tours of the town right now. I don't have the means to let you in."

"Oh, what a shame…"

"Okay, come on, Maeve," her companion—Bob, I'm pretty sure she called him—says in a weary tone. "We'll just have to leave it. Why don't we go back to that little boutique you liked?"

"Well, wait a moment. Maybe the lad can tell us something about the history of this place?" She turns back to me with hopeful eyes and I feel an impulse to help in some way, even though I'm completely underequipped to do so.

"Sure…" They both seem delighted, and I immediately regret the impulse as I cast about in my mind for the limited information I know about this place. "Well, this is the original blacksmith's from when the town was first established during the gold rush." That much I *do* know. Maeve and Bob nod in interest, encouraging me to continue. "Um...it's where all the locals' tools were made back then, and right into the twentieth century until mass machinery took over." I scan my eyes around the site as I try desperately to recall all the other pieces of history that have been forced on me over the years, but my patience for all those old stories was always pretty much nonexistent and it seems I've managed to push them all out of my brain. "Um...there was a murder. Right here," I blurt out, pointing to a random spot right near the entrance to the blacksmith's. I have no idea if that's true, but it sounds exciting and definitely plausible.

Bob and Maeve's eyes widen simultaneously. "A *murder?*" Maeve gasps. "What happened?"

I nod, spurred on by their enthusiasm. "It was tragic, really. A young woman was bludgeoned to death with the blacksmith's tongs back in 1889."

Maeve puts a hand to her mouth. "How awful! Why was she killed?"

I shrug. "No one knows why for sure. But there's a theory that her husband—the blacksmith, himself—didn't want her running off to join the circus."

Next to me, and out of sight of the tourists, I can see Zack shaking with silent laughter. It's taking everything I have to keep my expression somber and regretful right now.

"The *circus?*" Maeve exclaims.

I nod. "That's what they say. Apparently her husband didn't want her to leave him alone with their five kids. Which, when you think about it, makes killing her a completely idiotic move."

Bob shakes his head in dismay. "Well, they weren't too bright back then, were they?"

I fold my arms over my chest, feeling mildly satisfied with myself. "No, they sure weren't."

After Bob and Maeve bid goodbye and wander off, presumably to visit Livia's boutique, I step back behind the partition, wasting no time in getting my hands back on Zack's body.

"So…blowjob?"

"Maybe we could move away from the murder scene?" Zack suggests with a teasing quirk of his lips.

I let out a soft chuckle and grab his hand. "Come on. My place."

13

From the private Facebook group 'Finchley Locals Community Hangout'

Post by Missy Clarke: I saw Zack and Slater walking down main street ARM IN ARM yesterday! And today Zack's rental car was parked outside Slater and Chance's house for quite a long time. I think this could be it. Zater is back on!!!
Chance Kingsley reply to Missy Clarke's post: How do you know about the rental car? Have you been staking out our house??
Missy Clarke reply to Chance Kingsley's comment: Of course not. Your house happens to be on my daily walking route
Gunner Clarke reply to Missy Clarke's post: Mom, you're getting way too excited about this. It's embarrassing. More embarrassing than usual I mean *eye roll emoji*

***Missy Clarke** reply to **Gunner Clarke**'s comment:* What? When do I embarrass you?

***Gunner Clarke** reply to **Missy Clarke**'s comment:* Please don't make me get out the list

***Candace Goode** reply to **Missy Clarke**'s post:* 'Zater'? Was that a thing?

***Rock Goode** reply to **Missy Clarke**'s post:* When did this group become Gossip Girl?

***Jesse Cartwright** reply to **Rock Goode**'s comment:* Where the hell have you been, man? The gossip's the only reason I'm here

Zack

"So…?" Jesse asks, fixing me with an expectant look.

I shake my head in feigned ignorance. "So, what?"

Jesse just lets out an annoyed grunt and slumps back against the booth seat across from me. Next to him, Lawson lets out a soft chuckle.

"So…what's going on with Slater? That's what I think he's trying to ask," Lawson supplies.

I give a one-shouldered shrug and concentrate on dipping a fry into my salt and pepper dip. "Nothing's going on. You shouldn't believe everything you hear."

Jesse lets out a disbelieving snort. "That'd be a lot more convincing if your neck wasn't covered in hickeys."

My hand immediately flies to cover my neck as my

mind flashes back to this afternoon and Slater sucking and biting at my skin as he pounded inside me. *Damn Slater and his stupid awesome lips...*

I stare across at Lawson and Jesse, both of them wearing expressions of amused expectation and looking as though they could sit there all night waiting for me to 'fess up. Finally, I snap. "Okay, fine! We're fucking, okay?" I cry, throwing my hands in the air.

And, of course, because it's me and I've always been known for my expert timing, that pronouncement comes right as there's a lull in the conversations around us. My face flames as what feels like every single person in the saloon turns their gaze my way.

Across the room, Slater is hanging at the bar with George, Axel, and Chance. He catches my eye and offers an incredibly self-satisfied smirk that makes me want to hurl one of Lawson's pickles at him. Instead, I just sink down in my booth and stare at my mostly-empty plate, attempting to avoid eye contact with everyone around me.

"I always thought it'd only be a matter of time before you guys figured your shit out," Jesse comments.

I lift my gaze to glare at my brother. "We haven't figured anything out. It's just sex."

Jesse shrugs in a way that tells me he's not remotely convinced by that statement.

My glare intensifies. "Shouldn't you be getting all overprotective and warning me away from him right now?"

Jesse takes a sip of his soda, his features creased in confusion. "Why?"

I let out an aggravated sigh. "Because you're my big brother. You're supposed to do stuff like that. Warn me away from the guy who broke my heart et cetera, et cetera…"

Jesse just waves away my comment. "You're a big boy. I'm sure you're over all that by now."

That prompts Lawson to let out a loud snort of laughter, which he unsuccessfully tries to hide by taking a quick sip of his drink.

Jesse's gaze flicks to my best friend, before turning back to me, his mouth hanging open in incredulity. "You've got to be kidding me. It's been *twelve* years, Zack. You were kids. Don't you think it's time to move on?"

I sit up and lean forward over the table, pinning my brother with a hard look. "I have two words for you: Webster Goode."

"That's a completely different situation," Jesse snaps in a voice so scathing it prompts me to rear back in my seat. I start to open my mouth to ask for about the billionth time what the fuck happened between those two back in high school, but then Jesse starts talking again. "Besides, did it ever enter your mind that maybe Slater made the right call all those years ago?"

I stare at my brother, completely numb with a mix of shock and betrayal. "What the fuck are you talking about?"

Jesse lets out a heavy sigh. "Come on, Zack. You were eighteen. Do you honestly think you could have done long distance for four years? "

"I—" My mouth opens and closes as I struggle to form the words running through my head. *We* would have made it work. *We* could have done it. If we'd just had the chance...

"And don't forget *you* were the one who chose to go to Chicago for school," Jesse points out. "You could have gone to Davis, or even Berkley would have been closer..."

"Wow. Great to know you're on my side," I mutter, scowling down at my plate.

"Fucking hell, it's not about sides," Jesse growls. "I just don't want to see you throw away something that could be really great because you're too stubborn to let go of this grudge."

I feel my hackles rising; I can barely even look at Jesse as my entire body thrums with a burning tension I don't know what to do with. I scan my eyes about the room again and find that everyone has well and truly returned to their dinners and conversation, and at the bar Slater and the others have now been joined by Tansie and Web.

With a sigh, I slide out of the booth and get to my feet. Leaning over the table, I say to Jesse, "I don't know what the hell happened between you and Web, but you're the *last* person who gets to lecture me about hanging onto grudges." I straighten up and toss some cash down for my meal before adding, "Besides, I already told you it's just sex. You need to stop reading all that crap in the Facebook group."

Before he has a chance to respond, I turn and weave my way around the tables, heading for the street.

SLATER

"Seriously, could you be more obvious?" George asks with a smirk as he pulls a beer from the tap, sliding it across the bar in Axel's direction.

"I'm sure he probably could be," Chance says with a loud chuckle and a slap on my back. "He could jump up on one of the tables and sing a Katy Perry song like he did when he invited Zack to prom."

"It was Taylor Swift, straight boy," I correct.

"Potato, potahto," Chance says with a wave of his hand. "It was all pretty *Glee*, whatever it was."

"That happened before *Glee* started," George points out.

Chance arches an eyebrow at my cousin. "The fact you know when *Glee* started is a little concerning, man."

"What's concerning about that?" George asks, his expression one of faux-obliviousness. "I think you should be concerned that you find it concerning."

"Can we *please* stop talking about *Glee*," Axel grumbles, taking a sip of his beer.

"Yeah, let's talk about how Slater can't keep his eyes off Zack," Chance practically shouts before staring as unsubtlety as humanly possible at the booth where Zack's currently eating dinner with his brother and Lawson.

"Please, say it louder, I beg of you," I mutter.

"Well, if you're going to sit there stinking up my saloon with all your pheromones you could at least give us some details," George says after returning from serving another customer.

I let out a wry breath of laughter. "Yeah, that won't be happening."

"Why not? I always share details about my love interests. The least you could do is reciprocate."

My brows shoot up at the sheer ridiculousness of the statement. "Okay, firstly, you don't have love interests, you have sexual conquests. And, secondly, you don't *share* details, you *inflict* them. No matter how many times we tell you we don't want to hear about Stacey and the thing with the maple syrup, or Kelly Anne and the weird doll three-way, or—"

"Chloe and the vibrator that got stuck," Axel says, practically taking the words from my mouth.

"Or—"

I shake my head, cutting Chance off before he can add to the list of George's sexual adventures. "Don't you start, you're just as bad."

Chance's mouth falls open in horror. "I've never had a doll three-way in my life!"

"Dude, you haven't lived," George says with a grin, before peeling away from the bar to serve a customer at the other end.

I take a sip of my beer and sneak another glance across the saloon at Zack, my chest tightening as I catch sight of him grinning at something Jesse's saying. Jesus, he has such an incredible smile…

To be honest, the main reason I don't want to go into detail about what's happening between Zack and me— apart from the whole it not being anyone else's business thing—is because I still have no idea where we stand.

It's been two days since we decided to have some no-strings-attached fun while Zack's in town, and, trust me, that's been great. Really, really great. It's not exactly what I want, though. I want strings—*all* the strings. But Zack's leaving on Thursday and, as far as I know, his mind hasn't budged at all.

George returns to our little group and pulls a new beer for me, replacing the one I've just finished.

As he slides it across the bar, from the other side of the room I hear Zack practically shout, "Okay, fine! We're fucking, okay?"

It seems as though every single person in the saloon turns their attention first to Zack, and then straight to me. Including the guys I'm hanging with.

"Well, I guess that answers that question," Ax says with a gruff chuckle.

George shrugs. "You never know. He could be talking about someone else…"

"I doubt it," I say, unable to keep the smile off my face. The amount of hours Zack and I have spent in bed, or against the wall, or in the tray of my truck, or—well, you get the picture—over the past couple days, I can't see him finding either the time or energy to be with someone else. And, hell, call me cocky but I can't see him wanting to—I know how to keep a guy satisfied.

It's not long after Web's arrived that I return from the bathroom to find Zack is no longer at his table.

"He left," George tells me before I've even opened my mouth to ask the question. "Just a few moments ago. He looked in kind of a mood."

Barely pausing to bid goodbye to my brother and

cousins, I make my way out of the saloon in search of Zack.

I find him just outside, kicking at the pavement in a gesture I find endearingly familiar.

"Hey."

Clearly startled, he spins around to face me, eyes wide with surprise. "Hey."

"You want to go somewhere?" I ask.

He arches an eyebrow. "Is the place your bed?"

I let out a soft chuckle. "Tempting, but I was actually thinking of somewhere else."

Zack considers the offer for a moment before shrugging a shoulder and gesturing for me to lead the way.

My truck is parked just a little way down Main Street from the saloon; when I lead us there, I'm half-expecting Zack to protest or ask questions about where we're going that we need to drive. But he doesn't, he just hops in the passenger seat and starts fiddling with the radio controls. I'm hit with a blast of memory from all the times he used to ride shotgun in my car when we were kids, and it takes me a moment to shake it off.

It's not until we're halfway to our destination that Zack says, "This is the way to the lake…"

I nod. "Yep

Technically, Dewer Lake is more of a stream, as it's not landlocked and is actually connected to the American River, but the part we go to is enclosed by an ancient rock formation that slows the current to the point where it's basically non-existent. It's an incredibly beautiful place, and is perfect on late summer afternoons when the water's been warmed through the day.

Even though it's after seven right now, there's still a good couple hours of light left in the day, and the best thing about going at this time of night is that there shouldn't be anyone else there. Which is a good thing considering I don't have a swimsuit and I'm pretty sure Zack doesn't either.

When we get to the lake, I do a quick check to make sure we are, in fact, alone, and then I scramble out of my clothes, folding them haphazardly and setting them on a rock. Zack's more careful about how he folds his, but nevertheless, after a minute or so we're both climbing carefully over the smooth boulders that encircle the swimming hole before diving into the tepid water.

"God, I forgot how amazing this place is," Zack says, his eyes alight with wonder as he gazes at the surroundings. "I haven't been here for forever."

"That can happen when you only come home, like, twice in a decade," I tease.

For a second I think maybe I've gone too far with the guilt, but then he just smirks and throws his hands down into the water, sending a wave in my direction and completely soaking me. With an elated cackle, he swims off out of reach.

"Oh, you are *so* going to pay!" I call out, chasing after him.

I catch up to him, flinging my arms around his waist and tackling him into the water. We wrestle for a bit and come up laughing like absolute crazy people.

"I love the sound of your laugh," I tell him, tickling him some more and watching him giggle and squirm.

His legs find their way around my waist, and the

laughter dies as his lips descend on mine, his fingers tugging at my wet hair.

I grip his ass tight, holding him against me as I snap my hips forward, grinding our cocks together.

"Fuck, Slater..." Zack groans, tearing his lips from mine and kissing all over my jaw and neck. He moves his hands to run down my body, gripping my hips tight and urging me to rut against him even more frantically.

"Jesus...so good, baby," I murmur breathlessly. "Always so fucking good with you."

Our lips crash back together again in a wild, desperate kiss that has me seeing stars. There's no one that kisses the way Zack does. No one.

Moving on instinct, barely conscious of what I'm doing, I slide my fingers between his cheeks and tease around his hole for a bit before eventually pushing inside. It drives him absolutely nuts, and he writhes against me, clinging desperately to my body and letting out groan after groan as I find his magic spot.

I feel his ass clamping down around my finger and his whole body goes tense in my arms as he hits his climax.

"Fuck, Slater, I'm...uhh..."

I withdraw my finger from his ass and he slips from my grip, his legs falling from around my waist so he's back standing on the silty floor of the stream. Then he wraps his hand around my cock, stroking it firmly as he tickles my balls with his other hand.

"Fucking hell," I hiss through my teeth, before letting out a rumbled groan as Zack swipes his thumb over the head of my cock. "Jesus."

"You like that?" he teases.

"You fucking know I do," I gasp out, barely managing to even form the words. With the amount of hand jobs we exchanged back in high school both of us are pretty damn familiar with what the other does and doesn't respond to.

Case in point: it only takes about a minute of Zack's expert ministrations for my orgasm to burn through me. I cling to his shoulders to steady myself, letting out a harsh groan as I explode into the water.

After I've taken a second to gather my breath, I wrap my hands around his face and seal my lips over his, kissing him soft and slow. I want to tell him exactly what I'm feeling, but I know he doesn't want to hear it. So I settle for saying it with the kiss instead and tell myself that's enough.

14

From the private Facebook group 'Finchley Locals Community Hangout'

Post by Tansie Goode: Does anyone know anything about a woman who was murdered by the blacksmith in the 1800s? Some tourists said they heard the story from one of the locals?

Missy Clarke reply to Tansie Goode's post: No, that can't be right. Finchley's a nice, safe town. We wouldn't get murders here

Alice Ackerman reply to Missy Clarke's comment: You call this safe? My Fifi was violated in her own home!

Gunner Clarke reply to Alice Ackerman's comment: I thought female dogs wanted to have sex when they're in heat?

Alice Ackerman reply to Gunner Clarke's comment: So you're saying this is HER fault?? That she was ASKING FOR IT??

Gunner Clarke reply to Alice Ackerman's comment:
Okay I am sooo not getting sucked down this rabbit hole

Zack

I'M GETTING a little too used to waking in Slater's bed. I've never done the no strings attached thing before, but I'm pretty sure one of the big rules is that you're not supposed to sleep over. You're supposed to have sex, then split—no cuddling allowed. I'm sure if I asked Lawson he'd verify that for me.

But Slater and I haven't really been following that particular rule. There's just something that feels completely natural about falling into bed together after sex. I like the way his arms feel wrapped around me, the way his hot breath tickles my neck. And the scent of him…I love that familiar scent of wood shavings and furniture polish that just seems to linger all the time, as if it's being expelled from his skin.

There's nothing *wrong* with enjoying this part of our arrangement. It's not as though snuggling together suddenly makes us a couple. What it comes down to is that I'll be heading back to Chicago in a matter of days, and Slater will be staying here. This week will just be as he said on Saturday—a fun vacation fling. But I see no reason why I should deprive myself of awesome cuddle-time just because there's an expiry date on this thing.

"I can hear your brain whirring," Slater murmurs, his hot breath on the back of my neck making me tingle all over. "Why is your brain whirring at four thirty in the morning."

I turn to face him, the corner of my mouth quirking up as I catch sight of his sleepy expression. "No reason in particular."

He doesn't push back at my non-answer, which I'm glad about. I know what he really wants is for us to actually get back together, to be a proper couple again; but I can't do that. Sex is one thing, but I can't let him back into my heart. So I'm relieved that he doesn't urge me to confess how much I love cuddling with him; he doesn't need the encouragement.

"You know what I've been thinking about?" he asks with a sexy smile, lifting a hand to slide over my hip. "How much I still don't know about you."

My brows draw together in confusion, because I totally thought he was about to say something else. "What?"

He nods. "Yep. I know how much you love it when I kiss your neck. And when I play with your balls. And I know *exactly* how to make you scream when I'm inside you. But there's still so much I don't know about you. So much I've missed over the past twelve years."

I pull away from him and sit up, managing to curb the little voice that wants to scream at him *'And who's fault is that?'* Instead, I just sit there for a moment, waiting for the tension to ease out of my body. But it doesn't.

"What's wrong?" Slater asks warily.

I get off the bed and start rummaging on the floor for my clothes. As I tug my jeans on, I fix him with a hard look. "This is supposed to just be sex, Slater."

"I know that." He's trying to be casual but there's a slight edge to his voice that reveals just how frustrated he is with the situation.

"Right. Then why do you keep going on about how much you've missed, and how you don't know me anymore? What does it matter? This will be over in a few days anyway."

"Don't you usually like to know the person you're sleeping with?" he challenges.

"I—"

I'm not sure what I was planning to say, but it doesn't matter because Slater cuts me off with a heavy sigh, before murmuring, "Maybe we shouldn't wait the extra few days…"

I blink at him in surprise, both at his words and at the way every cell in my body seems to be rebelling upon hearing them. "You want to end this now?"

He merely shrugs. "To be honest, I've got a busy few days coming up—I'm not sure how much time I'll have anyway."

I nod, feeling a little numb. "Yeah. Okay. Makes sense." I grab my t-shirt from the floor before tugging it on and heading for the door. "I guess I'll see you around."

It takes me all of three minutes to drive back to my mom's place, texting Lawson as soon as I get in the door.

LAWSON HALE: *WHAT DO YOU MEAN YOU JUST GOT DUMPED? I THOUGHT YOU GUYS WERE JUST MESSING AROUND?*

Me: *So did I! It was just sex, I swear! I made that very clear from day one*

Me: *But it feels like a dumping!*

Lawson Hale: *Dude, if it feels like a dumping then it wasn't just sex*

Fuck. I toss my phone down and flop onto my bed. Lawson's right. I should feel completely indifferent right now; or, worst case, like I've just had my ego crushed a little.

But that's not what's going on. I feel…sad. Not angry, or bitter, just…sad. Like I've lost something really special, and I don't understand how it happened or what I'm supposed to do next.

※

I'm still in a complete funk the next day, but I manage to pull myself out of bed and head into town. I tell myself it's not in the hopes of at least getting a glimpse of Slater, but that's a damn lie.

I'm sitting at one of the tables in the saloon, working on some stuff for Lawson, when George takes the seat opposite me. Of course, he doesn't sit normally, instead turning the chair around and straddling it as though he's a character in a '90s sitcom.

"Hey, man, sorry to interrupt," he says with a sheepish grin. "I just caught a glimpse of your screen and saw you're doing some stuff for Lawson. You mind if I give you some feedback on his books?"

I blink at him a few times as my brain struggles to

process the direction of this conversation. "You read one of Lawson's books?"

He nods eagerly. "Not just one. I read all the *Drake Porter* books. They were great, although I thought he let himself down a little when it came to the sex."

"How so…?" I ask, still a little baffled.

"Well, it was a bit dull, to be honest. There just wasn't much chemistry there."

"Uh huh." I give a nod, before carefully asking, "Do you think perhaps the fact that you're straight might have something to do with you not liking sex scenes between two men?"

George shakes his head adamantly. "Nah, that's not what I mean. Of course it didn't turn me on—I was expecting that. But the characters went from having oodles of chemistry everywhere else in the book to having absolutely none when it came to the sex stuff. It just didn't feel believable."

My head feels like it's about to explode from the sheer absurdity of this conversation. This must be how women feel when men try to mansplain to them.

Before I can respond, George holds his hand up in a somewhat placating gesture. "I don't mean to say it's not *accurate*," he clarifies. "I have no way of knowing if it is or not, but I get the impression Lawson's done a fair bit of field research so I'll take his word on all the mechanics of everything…"

"Well, at least there's that," I say dryly.

"All I'm trying to say is it felt a little flat. Porter and Agent Scott had this really intense, fiery relationship throughout the rest of the books, but the sex didn't feel like a natural progression of that. It felt like it was just jammed in there. No pun intended," he adds with a smirk.

I roll my eyes, and am just about to respond to this latest spiel when I catch sight of Lawson entering the saloon.

"William Shakespeare here thinks your sex scenes don't have enough chemistry," I say as Lawson takes a seat on the chair next to mine.

Law merely offers George a friendly smile, one shoulder lifting in a small shrug. "I've had other readers mention that as well. It's something I'm trying to work on for the next book."

My mouth falls open in surprise. "He was *right?*"

Lawson shrugs again. "Apparently."

"Why didn't I pick up on it then?" I ask, my brow creased in agitation. I'm Lawson's alpha reader, I'm supposed to spot problems like this.

George chuckles. "My guess is you got distracted by all the cocks flying around the place. I didn't have that problem."

"You want to be an alpha reader for my next book?" Lawson offers, making me almost fall off my chair in shock.

George's face lights up. "Seriously? I get to read it before everyone else?"

"You'll get it at the same time as Zack," Lawson clarifies.

"Oh my god, yes! That would be so awesome," George rambles, his face lit up with amazement. "Dude, your books are so amazing—I can't wait to read the next one!"

I grin as I catch Lawson's cheeks flaring pink from the

praise. But it slips from my face pretty quickly when I realize this is the first time since yesterday morning that I've actually managed to smile.

Fucking Slater. Why on earth did I think it was a good idea to jump down that rabbit hole?

15

From the private Facebook group 'Finchley Locals Community Hangout'

Post by Raymond 'Sheriff' Taylor: A complaint has been made about someone failing to respect the town's poop scooping guidelines. Fines will be issued to anyone found not scooping after their dog poops

Hank Latham reply to Raymond 'Sheriff' Taylor's post: Who is this person? We deserve names!

Alice Ackerman reply to Hank Latham's comment: I'm not sure you should be getting all high and mighty Hank. Mabel is the worst poop offender!

Hank Latham reply to Alice Ackerman's comment: Mabel has an exemption, I can show you the paperwork from the mayor!

"Why the fuck would you go and do something idiotic like that?" Web growls after I've finally come clean about breaking things off with Zack.

I let out a sigh of frustration. "Things were going to end tomorrow anyway. He wasn't about to change his mind about going back to Chicago."

Web lets out a disapproving grunt and I turn to Chance, appealing for him to say something reasonable.

He just shakes his head. "Don't look at me. I'm with him," he says, gesturing to Web. "You're an idiot."

I let out a frustrated groan and fall into one of the chairs in front of Chance's desk. "Can we just do this, please? I have a job to get back to."

Chance nods and shuffles some papers on his desk. "Yes, absolutely. Mrs. Ackerman will be in shortly—I don't want to keep her waiting."

Web chuckles softly and takes the chair next to me. "Who's dog is she suing this time?"

The corner of Chance's mouth curves into a wry grin. "Lawyer-Client confidentiality. Sorry." He lays out the papers we need to sign on the desk in front of us and sets a pen on top. "Everything's marked where you need to initial and sign. Nothing's changed since you read through them last week."

I nod and take the contract and the pen, quickly scanning through it and signing where noted. Then I hand it to Web for him to do the same.

"Congratulations, boys. You're in business," Chance

says with a bright smile once Web hands him back the contract.

I let out a breath of wry laughter. It's going to take more than a signature on a piece of paper for us to actually get the businesses merged together but at least now we can move forward with the rest of it.

After leaving Chance's office, I decide to head over to Nanna's as it's been a few days since I've visited.

When she opens the door, instead of her usual friendly smile, I get a disapproving frown. "I heard you broke things off with Zack again."

My mouth falls open in shock and I just stand there for a moment before finally shaking it off and stepping inside, closing the door behind me. "How the hell did you even know that? No one was even supposed to know we were…well…whatever it was."

Nanna shrugs. "The whole town knows. You know what it's like here." She looks thoughtful for a moment. "Maybe people have hidden cameras or something…I wouldn't put it past Missy Clarke, that's for sure."

I let out a soft breath of laughter, shaking my head in wry amusement. As gossipy and intrusive as Missy can be sometimes, I know in reality she's completely harmless.

"So, is it true?" Nanna demands, hands placed firmly on her hips. "Did you really ditch that poor boy *again.*"

"What the hell is with everyone?" I say with a groan. "Why can't they just stay out of my life?"

Her demeanor morphs into something more resembling sympathetic. "They all just care about you, angel. As do I. None of us want to see you make the same mistake you did twelve years ago."

I let out a heavy sigh. "Why am I always the one making the mistake? He's the one who's always leaving—why don't you give him one of your talking tos?"

Nanna shrugs. "He's not my grandson."

I roll my eyes at her biased logic. "Look, I'm sorry to disappoint everyone, but clearly Zack and I just aren't meant to be together. His life is in Chicago now and he's made it abundantly clear he wants to go back to it."

"Has he?" Nanna asks, one eyebrow raised. "Does he talk about Chicago a lot?"

I frown in thought for a moment. "Well...not exactly..." *He just keeps talking about leaving...*

"Maybe you need to give him a reason to stay," she suggests, as if it were that simple.

"It's not that easy, Nanna," I say in a weary voice. Why do people keep acting like this is something that can just be fixed with a snap of the fingers?

"It *is* that easy," she says firmly. "You love the man. Tell him what he means to you before he leaves. And if he leaves anyway, well at least you'll know you tried." She reaches out and takes my hands, rubbing them gently as she looks up at me with an entreating gaze. "Trust me, angel. You don't want to leave anything unsaid. Life's far too short."

I let my eyes fall closed, hearing the significance of Nanna's words loud and clear. With a soft sigh, I offer a nod of acquiescence. "Okay. I'll talk to him."

Nanna's face lights up with a wide grin. "Good boy," she says, gently patting the back of my hand.

Considering Nanna's place is right next door to Zack's mom's, where he's been staying for his visit to Finchley, I don't waste any time after finishing up my visit with Nanna before crossing the front lawn and knocking on the Cartwright's front door.

"Hey," Zack says upon answering. There's a startled expression on his face, as though I'm pretty much the last person he expected to see here. *I guess that's fair.*

"Hey. Um...can I talk to you?"

He nods, still looking confused and maybe a little... hopeful? Or is that just wishful thinking getting the better of me? "Yeah, okay. Come on in." He stands aside and gestures for me to enter the house.

"Is anyone else around?" I ask warily.

He shakes his head. "Mom's at work and Jesse went home this morning."

I nod and follow him inside.

"Should I be worried you don't want any witnesses around?" Zack teases, arching an eyebrow at me.

I let out a soft chuckle. "I just want us to talk privately. That's all."

When we get to the kitchen at the back of the house, Zack turns to face me. "So...what do you want to talk about?"

I hesitate for a moment, trying to find my words. I've never really been great with words—that was always Zack's department—so rather than making some grand, sweeping speech, I decide to start with something simple. "I'm sorry about yesterday." When he doesn't say anything, I continue, "Look, I know what I said about this thing just being a casual, vacation fling. But I also know that you know I never actually meant that." I pause for a moment, waiting for him to nod. "I thought I could be cool about the whole thing and just take whatever you'd give me, but yesterday with all that talk about leaving, it just…hit a nerve. And I kind of overreacted," I finish with a shrug.

"*I* hit a nerve?" he asks incredulously. "You're the one who ended things back then."

"Because you were leaving," I throw back, not realizing until this moment just how much hurt I've been carrying around about his decision to go to school so far away.

"We were going to do long distance."

I let out a soft sigh, shaking my head. "*When* has long distance ever worked?"

Fixing me with the kind of intense look that makes me stagger back a step, he says, "*We* would have made it work. Because it was *us*. You and me. *We* could have done it, Slater. But then *you* decided it wasn't enough. You decided to give up before we even tried."

"I did what I thought was best," I say softly.

"And broke my fucking heart in the process," Zack says, bitterness evident in his tone.

I have to glance away for a moment, drawing in a deep breath as I let the weight of his words settle over me. Does he think my heart wasn't in pieces as well? Making that decision almost ended me. Not to mention what happened a few weeks later…

Finally, I manage to meet Zack's gaze again, my voice hoarse as I say, "For someone with such a broken heart, you seemed to move on pretty damn fast."

Zack shakes his head, his brows drawn in confusion. "What the hell are you talking about?"

I sigh. "It took me all of a week to realize what a

fucking idiot I'd been, and then another two to work up the nerve to come see you at school."

"You never came to see me at school…"

I nod, insisting, "I did. And I saw you with a guy. You seemed…happy. Really happy. And it was clear to me you'd moved on. I figured I'd already hurt you enough, I didn't want to get in the way of you being happy." I glance away, my throat tight as I continue, "That's all I wanted for you. So, as much as it killed me, I walked away."

Zack blinks at me a few times, his expression still full of confusion. "Slater, I don't know what you're talking about. I wasn't dating anyone those first few weeks of college."

I shake my head adamantly. "I saw you," I insist. "It was a tall guy. He was wearing a red hoodie and a Blackhawks cap, and he had his arm around you. And you were just… so happy."

Zack stares at me for a long moment, before throwing his hands up in frustration and crying, "Jesus Christ, Slater. That was Lawson!"

My brow furrows in confusion as I try to think back to that day. Surely it couldn't have been…I would have recognized him…

But as I picture that guy and then mentally add twelve years, I realize it's true. The likeness is unmistakable.

Zack must see the realization on my face, because he lets out a soft groan and throws his head back. "You've got to be kidding me. Are you actually telling me if it weren't for Law we'd have worked all this shit out twelve years ago?"

I offer a hesitant smile. "Is that you admitting you'd have taken me back?"

He shakes his head wryly and steps toward me. His eyes are narrowed, but there's a hint of a smile curving his lips. "I like to think I would have made you grovel. A lot. But, truthfully, I'd have taken you back in a second."

I move even closer, resting my hands at his waist and tilting my head down to catch his lips in a soft kiss. I still have no idea where this is going—if it's even going anywhere—but if he's leaving tomorrow I plan to make the most of every moment we have tonight.

"Come with me," I tell him, linking my fingers through his and leading him toward the door.

"Where?"

I offer a secretive smile. "You'll see."

16

Post by Chance Kingsley: Due to a recent uptick in my caseload I will no longer be taking on animals as clients

Alice Ackerman reply to Chance Kingsley: But Fifi needs representation! She's about to lose her children!

Missy Clarke reply to Alice Ackerman's comment: I feel for you, Alice. It's just like that movie with Sally Field *crying emoji*

Beth Bowry reply to Missy Clarke's comment: If you're talking about Not Without My Daughter I think you need to give that a re-watch Missy

Irene Henderson reply to Chance Kingsley's post: Will you still take cases with an animal defendant? My fish has been looking at me real funny lately. I don't think it's coincidence my arthritis is playing up worse than before!

Zack

"Should I be worried that you might taking me to some far off location to kill me?" I joke as Slater drives us farther away from town.

He grins. "Don't worry. If I were planning to kill you, I wouldn't be driving to a property I own. That's just a huge smoking gun."

My brows shoot up. "You own property out here?"

"Uh huh."

I take a new interest in the landscape outside my window. It's hard to see in the dark, but it appears we're driving past a series of vineyards and apple orchards. I know Slater's uncle Rock owns an orchard about twenty-five minutes outside town; I wonder if we're headed anywhere near there.

"Is your property near Rock's?"

"Yeah, it's on his land. Or, at least, what used to be his land," Slater explains. "He divided a little section off and sold it to me a few years ago."

After a few more minutes, Slater turns off the highway and onto a dirt road that even in the dark I can recognize as the entrance road to Crimson Grove, Rock's orchard. But instead of driving all the way to the gate, Slater veers off again, this time onto an even rockier path that tests the no doubt excellent suspension of his truck's tires.

We finally pull up in front of a two-story weather-board house that seems somehow both familiar and completely foreign at the same time. Slater turns off the engine and we get out of the truck. Glancing around at my surroundings, I strain through the darkness to try to get my bearings, attempting to figure out what seems so familiar about this place. And, finally, it hits me.

"Oh my god. Is this the haunted house?"

Slater chuckles. "Not haunted anymore. Not that it ever really was…"

This house was the original homestead on the orchard, dating back to gold rush times. For whatever reason, at some point in the twentieth century one of the previous owners decided they didn't like the position of this house and built a newer one way over on the other side of the property. This house had been left to basically rot, although when Rock bought the orchard he'd made sure it was at least safe enough for his nieces and nephews to hang out in there without fear of injury. Thinking back now, it probably wasn't the most child-friendly play area…but we all survived, so I guess that's the main thing.

My gaze is filtered by memory as I look up at the house. It has definitely changed a lot since the last time I saw it, which I have to assume is Slater's doing. From what I can see in the darkness, it no longer looks completely dilapidated on the outside, but rather a little unfinished. There's plastic sheeting covering one top corner and several windows, and there's a safety platform set up for the top floor. What is finished, though, looks new and pristine.

"Jeez, this looks amazing, Slater," I say, awe in my voice. "It's going to be incredible when it's done."

"Hopefully."

I tear my gaze from the house and offer a quirk of my lips. "Can I see inside?"

"It's not really safe inside. Half the floor is missing."

I step toward him, reaching out to run my hands down his sides. "Damn, and here I was hoping for a real-life *Notebook* moment."

He lets out a soft chuckle. "I can grow a beard if that'd make you happy."

A harsh growl escapes me and I bring my hands up to cup his cleanly-shaven cheeks. "Don't even think about it."

His lips are on mine in an instant, his arms circling my waist and tugging me close against him. I groan into his mouth as his tongue pushes past my lips to clash with mine. Heat consumes my entire body as we devour each other, my hands sliding into his hair and clinging tight. I couldn't let go right now if I wanted to.

Slater takes a few steps back, bringing me with him as he stumbles backward through the open passenger door of the truck and props himself on the seat. I try to climb up on his lap, but it's awkward and cramped, and even with Slater's hands on my ass I can't get a secure position.

Finally, he tears his lips from mine, letting out a groan of frustration. "Fuck. This isn't...we can't...not here..."

For a horrifying second, I think he's going to suggest we drive all the way back into town, but then he gently prompts me to hop back to the ground, before jumping down himself and grabbing my hand in a firm grip. He tugs me away from the truck and around the side of the house, where I can see a smaller structure about a hundred yards away. The old barn.

As we approach, I realize that, unlike the house, the

refurbishment of the barn has already been completed. It even has power connected, which is evident when Slater lets go of my hand to slide the giant door open, before taking a few steps to the side to flick a light switch.

As light floods the barn, I can see it's now very different to the old structure I remember. The ancient animal stalls are gone, as are all the holes in the wall and in the roof.

"This is my workroom," Slater says, gesturing to the area around us.

I offer a wry smile at his rather redundant words. From the wall of tools set up on one side, as well as the large oak workbench, not to mention several pieces of handcrafted furniture at the back of the room, I'd already guessed he wasn't using this space to host drag shows.

"It looks great," I tell him honestly. "But I thought you and Web were going into business together? Are you sharing this place?" It's definitely an impressive set up, but it doesn't really seem big enough for the kind of scale of projects Web and Slater have been talking about.

Slater shakes his head. "No, this is just for me. A side gig, or hobby, or whatever you want to call it."

I turn to face him, offering a smile full of all the pride and affection I'm feeling. "It's amazing."

His cheeks burn pink at my praise and he ducks his head modestly before lifting his gaze to mine again. His eyes are burning with the kind of anticipation that has nerves crackling through my whole body. "Come on. I haven't even shown you the best part." He takes my hand again and tugs me gently toward the back of the barn, letting go only when we get to the ladder that reaches up to the loft.

Slater climbs up and I follow after him, emerging to find what appears to be a little apartment. Wooden railing —no doubt handcrafted by Slater himself—adorns the loft's edge, all the way along except for a small opening for the ladder, giving the loft the feel of being completely separate from the rest of the barn despite the fact it's still open space. Like the room below, the loft has been completely refurbished, with hardwood floors, painted walls, down lights in the raked ceiling, and—judging by what I can see through the slightly cracked door—a small bathroom on one side. The rest of the space is a studio bedroom, complete with a neatly made queen bed.

After scanning my eyes around the room and taking everything in, I turn my gaze back to Slater, my brows raised. "You stay here often?"

The corner of his mouth quirks up. "I do, actually. I'm out here most weekends, either working on the house or in my workroom. Rock was really good about letting me crash at his place when I first started the house, but I like my own space…"

"Well, it's definitely pimped out pretty nicely."

He chuckles. "You should have seen it a few years ago. It was basically just a mattress and a sleeping bag."

My nose screws up in distaste. "Yeah, I'm not sorry I missed that."

Slater grins and steps toward me, linking his arms around my waist and pulling me close. "You know, I've always wanted to have sex up here," he murmurs, dropping his head to trail kisses along my jaw. "Ever since those hand jobs back in tenth grade."

I grin at the memory; we'd been hanging at the old house—drinking beer, if memory serves—and Slater and I had sneaked away from the group so we could fool around in the barn. Right here in this very loft.

His hands find their way to my ass and he urges me even closer. I groan at the feel of his hard cock pressing against mine, my arms flying up to clutch at his neck.

"As much as I hate all this time we've missed, I'm glad we waited to do it in a bed," Slater chuckles. I shudder in his arms as his hot breath tickles my neck. "Not that I wouldn't still want you if there wasn't one. Fuck, Zack..." He kisses my neck. "Any time, any place..." His lips move to my throat. "You're all I want."

I grab a fistful of Slater's hair and yank his head up, slamming my lips to his. He responds instantly, groaning into my mouth as the kiss deepens and our tongues twine together.

I'm barely cognizant of the fact that we're moving across the room, or that we're losing our clothing in the process; all I know is that I'm desperate for Slater. His lips, his skin, the heat of his body...I need it all, and I sure as hell can't focus on anything else right now. So when I'm tossed down and feel the soft landing of the mattress underneath me, I find myself staring up at Slater in surprise.

"We're on the bed."

His brows shoot up, the corner of his mouth quirking in a wry smile. "Yep."

I blink in confusion. "I don't remember moving to the bed."

He grins. "I'll take that as a compliment." He drops his head and claims my lips again.

I wrap my legs around his waist, lifting my hips to meet his downward thrusts as he grinds his cock against mine. My hands roam desperately over the bare skin of his back, feeling hard, rippling muscle under my fingertips.

I tear my lips from his, tossing my head back with a breathless groan. "Slate…Jesus…" I need to slow down. If we keep going like this I'm going to blow in a matter of minutes.

But slowing down isn't really Slater's style, and I've barely caught my breath before he's moving down my body and sliding his tongue around one of my nipples. *Fuck*…when did my shirt come off? When did *his* shirt come off?

I dash the thought away, groaning as he gently tugs my nipple between his teeth, one of his hands coming up to tease the other one.

"Jesus, Slater," I gasp. "I need…I need…"

He finally pulls off my nipple and lifts his head to cast me a sexy grin. "I know exactly what you need, babe."

I feel bereft for a moment when he rolls away from me, but I quickly realize it's only so he can rummage through a little cupboard that's set next to the bed, ultimately retrieving a bottle of lube. My brain clears enough for me to realize I'm still in my jeans, so I hastily scramble out of them and my boxer briefs just in time for Slater's return to the bed.

He stands by the bed just staring at me for a moment, his eyes full of appreciation and burning desire. "You are so fucking beautiful, Zack."

There's a hoarse quality to his voice that reveals an emotion I'm not sure I'm entirely comfortable with, so as wonderful as his words make me feel, I decide to brush past them for my own sanity. Sitting up, I reach for him and draw him toward me for a firm, heady kiss, and that's all it takes to spark Slater back into action.

He climbs back onto the bed with me, pushing me back against the mattress and trailing kisses over my body as he uses the lube to prep me.

"Damnit, that's enough!" I cry in a strangled gasp. "Please, Slate. Please, just…"

He offers me that sexy crooked smile again and drops one last kiss to my jaw before removing his fingers.

Then he quickly tugs off his jeans and briefs before kneeling on the bed. I let out a needy little whimper at the sight of his gorgeous cock, hard and leaking and ready to fill me in that perfect way. The sound prompts Slater's lips to curve up at the edges as he squeezes a little lube on his palm and uses it to slick up his cock.

Once he's ready, he reaches for me and pulls me toward him. "Come here."

I move without question, finding myself wrapped around Slater's kneeling body, my hands clutching fistfuls of his hair as he grips my ass and guides me onto his cock.

I bury my head in his neck as he fills me excruciatingly slowly, only loosening his hold on my ass once he's completely bottomed out.

"God damnit...you feel so perfect," he says with a harsh groan as he begins to move inside me.

"Fuck, Slater...*fuck...*" It's all I can manage to get out. Just a string of curses and Slater's name. I tug harder at his hair, dragging his lips to mine for a wild, desperate kiss that just seems to go on and on until we tear away from each other, panting for breath.

I can admit without a shadow of doubt the sex was never this good back in high school. We were teenagers for fuck's sake, of course it wasn't. But this sizzling electricity, the intensity of what we share between us—that's nothing new. It's something that, as much as I've tried to deny it over the years, I've only ever had with Slater. And I'm pretty sure I only ever will.

I dash the thought from my mind and claim his lips again, unable to stop myself from biting down as he thrusts up hard inside me. I swallow his groan and cling to him even tighter as I feel the fire building inside me, on the verge of exploding into an inferno.

"Jesus...Slate, I'm so close..."

He reaches between us and wraps his large hand around my dick, stroking in firm, fast movements until I completely lose control, digging my teeth into his neck as I come in a shuddering wave.

He gives me a brief moment of recovery before lifting me off his cock and tossing me back down on the bed. Then he shuffles across the mattress and swings one leg over my body so he's straddling my chest. I watch, mesmerized, as Slater pumps his hard cock, his entire body straining with the desperate need to come. I open my mouth wide in anticipation, and a few moments later he lets out a harsh groan as ribbons of cum shoot from his cock to paint my face. I slide my tongue out around my mouth, lapping up as much as I can reach, before reaching up to tug Slater to me for a messy kiss. He comes willingly, not caring that he's getting a face-full of his own cum.

LATER, after we've showered and gotten each other off again, I'm lying wrapped up in Slater's arms, thoroughly sated, when a thought occurs to me. "So…earlier when you said you've been wanting to have sex up here—you just meant with me, right?"

He's quiet for a moment before murmuring, "What do you mean?"

I shift around so I can face him. "Well, you must have had other guys up here, right?" I honestly have no idea why I'm asking considering the thought makes me want to throw up, but for some reason I just need to know.

Slater arches a brow in question. "What makes you say that?"

I shrug and lift a hand to motion vaguely in the direction of the little cupboard next to the bed. "You keep supplies here…"

The corner of Slater's mouth quirks up. "You don't use lube when you're jerking off?"

Well, that's a pretty logical and obvious explanation. Although, there's a simple reason it didn't occur to me right away. "I jerk off in the shower," I admit.

That prompts Slater to spring up so he's half hovering over me, his expression one of clear surprise. *"Still?"*

"What do you mean *still*?" I ask irritably.

He rolls his eyes. "You were jerking off in the shower back in high school. I figured you'd have moved on by now."

"What's wrong with the shower?" I demand. "It's perfect. You're already naked. There's no mess…"

"It's a waste of water," he chides.

I cringe. He has a point. Drought isn't something I've had to worry about over the past twelve years, but I really should be more sensitive to what the people here have been dealing with.

I offer a contrite smile, lifting a hand up to stroke his cheek. "If it's any consolation, since I've been back here you've kept me so satisfied I haven't really needed to jerk off."

Slater grins and drops a soft kiss to my lips. "It is."

He settles back on the bed next to me, wrapping his arms around me once again. "And for the record," he says, his eyes full of sincerity as they stare deep into mine, "I've never brought other guys back here. You're actually the first person to see this place since it's been finished. Apart from Rock, but he doesn't really count."

I tilt my forehead to rest against his, drawing in a deep breath and savoring the earthy scent of him. Even now, after sex and a shower he still somehow smells like wood shavings and varnish. It's the scent of my past, and maybe, possibly, my future…

There's nothing left for me in Chicago anymore. But here…there could be something here.

17

From the private Facebook group 'Finchley Locals Community Hangout'

Post by Charlotte Rowe: I'm very excited that Lawson Hale has decided to make Finchley his home while he writes his next book series! How exciting to have a famous author living amongst us!

Hank Latham reply to Charlotte Rowe's post: He can't be that famous. I've never heard of him

Missy Clarke reply to Charlotte Rowe's post: We already have an author in town. Bill wrote that book about stick insects, remember?

Charlotte Rowe reply to Missy Clarke's comment: Yes but Lawson's sold more than four copies of his books

Beth Bowry reply to Charlotte Rowe's post: What kind of books does he write?

Charlotte Rowe reply to Beth Bowry's comment: Romance

Alice Ackerman reply to Charlotte Rowe's comment: Are there naughty bits?

George Goode reply to Alice Ackerman's comment: There sure are Mrs. A. And Lawson's agreed to do a reading at the next Drinking and Knitting and Book Club meeting.

Alice Ackerman reply to George Goode's comment: Oh! Maybe Lawson and I could each take a role and act it out together?

George Goode reply to Alice Ackerman's comment: Umm...that would definitely be...interesting *thinking emoji*

Gloria Cartwright reply to Alice Ackerman: They're gay books Alice. The sex scenes are between two men

Jesse Cartwright reply to Gloria Cartwright: Sometimes three *wink emoji*

Slater

When I wake up with Zack sprawled across my chest, I'm a little disoriented by how bright it is in the room; my bedroom barely gets any natural light thanks to the large tree just outside my window. But then I realize we're at the barn, and that the light is streaming through the circular plantation shutters on the loft window, which I of course forgot to shut last night. But I'm not sure I can really be held accountable for that lapse considering I was a little distracted with...other things.

It's still pretty early, so I want to let Zack sleep, but if the sun creeps over any farther there's no chance of that happening. Moving carefully, I begin to slide out from underneath his hold so I can get up to close the shutters.

"Where are you going?" he grumbles, clutching tighter to my chest as though in protest.

Well, so much for that plan...

"I just need to close the shutters."

He shakes his head, his eyes still firmly shut. "Nope. You stay here. Cuddles."

I let out a soft breath of laughter and sink back onto the mattress, wrapping my arms tighter around him and pulling him as close as we can get.

"I love waking up next to you," he murmurs, prompting my heart to burst with a fiery glow. "I probably shouldn't, but I really, really do."

"Me too." Remembering Nanna's words from yesterday, I lift my hand to run through Zack's dark, silky hair as I finally find the courage to admit, "I love everything about you."

His eyes flutter open and, although he doesn't say it, I can see the same emotion reflected back at me. And that's enough for now.

"I'm supposed to be going home today," he murmurs, the words like a bucket of ice dousing my good mood. I'd completely forgotten it's Thursday today. "But I think I'm going to cancel my flight."

My eyes snap to Zack's, hardly daring to believe what he's saying. "What?"

He offers the softest of smiles. "I want to stay here. At least for a little while—a few weeks, maybe. I want to give us time to figure out what we want."

I arch an eyebrow at him. "I already know what I want."

"Okay, fine," he says, his eyes rolling toward the ceiling. "I need time to figure out what *I* want."

Well, it's not exactly what I wanted to hear, but at least he's not leaving. Yet. It feels more like a stay of execution than anything else if I'm being honest.

Despite my attempts to keep my thoughts in check, some of my disappointment must be showing on my face, because Zack reaches a hand up to cup my cheek, his gaze full of affection as he says, "I know I want *you*. I'm not remotely uncertain about that. It's just...it's been so long for us. And so much has happened this week..." he glances away for a moment, letting out a weighted breath. "I just need some time to figure my head out."

I nod. "I get it. Take whatever time you need—I'm not going anywhere."

He grins and tilts his head to cover my mouth with his; it's a soft, slow kiss, full of promises and possibility.

When we break apart, I grab Zack around the waist and flip him onto his back before flinging my leg over his body so I'm straddling his waist. "I have a question..."

Zack arches an expectant brow. "Yeah?"

"If you're not flying out this afternoon, does that mean we can stay in bed all day?"

"Don't you have to work? It's Thursday."

I grin. "Web can cover for me. He owes me from the time he got stuck down in Mexico for three days."

Zack's brows shoot up. "That sounds like an interesting tale.

"It is. But I'll save it for when we're not naked in bed together and all I can think about is sucking your cock."

"That's, um, totally...uh, okay..." Zack mumbles as I make my way down his beautiful body. The mumbling turns into a string of hissed curses as I swirl my tongue around his dick, and I can't help the soft chuckle that escapes me. My heart burns with the perfect familiarity of it all.

❅

IT'S BEEN a week since Zack decided to extend his stay in Finchley, and so far things are going well. That is to say, so far we've barely been apart from each other, except for when I'm at work. Even last weekend when I was doing some work on the house, Zack came with me and set himself up with his laptop in the loft so he could do some stuff for Lawson. I'm not sure how productive either of us was with all the 'personal breaks' we were taking, but it was nice to have him there.

And you know what's even nicer? Last night my sister Everley was talking about what she'd like to do for her birthday and Zack said he'd definitely be there. Everley's birthday is still over a month away! Throw in the fact that Zack's barely even mentioned Chicago in the past week and I'm thinking things are looking pretty good for Operation Get Zack to Choose Finchley.

It's early Friday morning and I'm pulling on my work pants while I watch mournfully as Zack stretches out like a lazy cat across my bed. *So* unfair that my job requires me to be up early. I'd love nothing more than to stay in bed with him for a few more hours.

"Hey, babe, can you pass me my phone?" he says through a yawn, motioning sleepily to the top of the dresser where he must have set his phone to charge last night.

For the record, Zack hasn't actually moved in with me, but he's spent so much time here over the past week it does kind of feel like he's living here sometimes. And I'm not going to complain about that.

I stride over to the dresser and unplug his phone, tossing it over to him before opening the top drawer and pulling out one of the new t-shirts Web and I had made with our company logo on it.

"Oh my god!"

I spin around, quickly tugging the t-shirt down over my head to see Zack's expression is one of stunned surprise as he stares at his phone.

"What is it?"

"I got a job," he says, his voice sounding a little distant.

I pause for a moment, my heart thundering in my chest as I register the implications of this announcement. Before I can do or say anything completely stupid, though, I manage to kick back into supportive boyfriend mode and paste a bright smile on my face. "That's awesome!" I stride over to the bed and wrap him in my arms, planting a kiss to his forehead. "So happy for you, baby."

I know there must be a catch because he starts rambling like a crazy person, a sure sign that he's nervous. "I can't believe it. I applied for this position months ago but they passed me over. Now apparently they've decided they want me. They want me to start Monday. That's only three days from now! You'd think they'd give a guy more notice, right? I mean, what, am I just expected to say how high as soon as they ask me to jump?"

I draw in a harsh breath at the word 'Monday'. That's *way* too soon. "That's...wow. They must really want you."

Zack nods absently. "It seems like it. And here I thought I'd been blackballed from every marketing firm in the city after what happened with Rick."

My teeth grind together at the mention of that asshole's name. I definitely haven't given up on my plans to track him down and inflict some bodily harm.

"Slater, You okay?"

"Huh? What?" I snap out of my thoughts of revenge to find Zack frowning at me in concern.

"You had a weird look on your face..."

I shake my head adamantly. "No, no, I'm fine." Offering the brightest smile I can manage, I say, "This is great, Zack. You deserve this."

"You really think it's great? I'd need to go back to Chicago..." he says a little warily.

I sit on the bed next to him, wrapping my arm around him. The last thing I want is for him to leave, but he can't make this decision about me. "I think you've worked really hard and now you're being given a great opportunity. And it's not like you'll have a huge adjustment when you get to Chicago. You've got all your friends there, and contacts, and your apartment. You're all set."

I feel him stiffen against me and I wonder what the hell I've said wrong. I was cool, wasn't I? Or was he able to detect that hint of bitterness in my voice when I uttered the word 'Chicago'? Despite having only ever been to the place once, and even then it was just to the university, I've never hated a city more—from their hockey team to their stupid deep dish pizza.

I pull my arm away and get to my feet; frankly, holding him like this is starting to hurt. Figuratively, of course. It hurts knowing I only have a couple more days left with him, and I just need a second or I'll end up breaking down and begging him to stay.

Be cool, Slater. Just be supportive. "Okay, so… Monday," I say with a clap of my hands and what must be history's fakest smile on my face. "Better get you on a flight—what are you thinking, Sunday morning or afternoon?" Maintaining my casual facade, I sit at the end of the bed and start tugging on my work boots.

"Actually, I think I should go tonight," he says.

My foot falls to the floor with a soft thud as I turn to stare at Zack, my mouth parted in surprise. "Tonight?"

"Yeah. It'd be good to have the weekend to settle back in."

It'd be good to have the weekend to say a proper goodbye, but yeah, whatever.

"Okay, yeah, makes sense," I say with a stiff nod, just barely able to get the words out.

He nods as well, tossing his phone aside and scrambling off the bed. He rummages through the clothing on the floor, quickly tugging on briefs and jeans. "Okay, I should probably get going," he says once he has a t-shirt over his head.

"*Now?*" My brows draw together. "It's not even light

out." I want to tell him to wait, that I don't need to go into work today, that I can spend the day with him if it's going to be our last one together. But my brain's feeling kind of foggy and my mouth can't seem to form the words.

And then it's too late.

Zack shrugs. "Yeah, but I've got a ton of packing to do and there are a lot of people I need to say goodbye to." He walks over to the door, leaving me standing there in stunned silence. At the threshold of the door, he turns back and says, "This was fun, Slate. I'm really glad we worked out all that stuff from before."

He casts me a smile that chisels cracks into my heart before he disappears out the door leaving me utterly shaken.

18

From the private Facebook group 'Finchley Locals Community Hangout'

Post by Missy Clarke: Does any one have an update on whether Zack is staying or leaving? I can't take much more of this anticipation!
George Goode reply to Missy Clarke's post: I know what you mean, I'm on the edge of my seat here!

Zack

"Okay, I need you to explain exactly what's going on here because I don't entirely understand," Lawson says in a slow, measured voice as though he's talking to an upset child. "A week ago you said you were giving it at least a month before deciding anything, but now you're rushing back to Chicago?"

"I told you—I got a job," I say, pulling clothes from my dresser and placing them into the suitcase I have laid out on my bed.

"But...I thought..."

I whirl around to face him. "You thought what?"

Lawson's brows shoot up and I know I must look half-mad right now, but I can't help it. I'm agitated, and confused, and a million other things I can't figure out. "Well, I thought you were staying so you and Slater could have some time to figure things out?"

"Yeah, well, so did I," I cry, throwing my arms up. "But then I tell him about this job and he just can't *wait* to get rid of me. He was like 'that's so awesome, and your whole life's in Chicago, and you'll slot right back in there, and I won't miss you at all!'"

Lawson arches a skeptical brow. "Those were his *exact* words?"

I shrug and return to my packing. "I may be paraphrasing a little."

"Uh huh. Z, I think you're reading way too much into this—it sounds like he was just trying to be supportive."

I pause in the motion of placing a pair of jeans in my case. Turning back to Lawson, I eye him curiously. "You think he was lying? That he really wants me to stay?"

Lawson lets out a heavy sigh. "I *think* you two should try talking to each other for once, instead of always trying to guess what the other's thinking."

. . .

Taking Lawson's advice, I decide to head over to Slater's place to talk things out. Truthfully, I don't *want* to move back to Chicago. I mean, it's nice to know there's a company out there that wants to hire me, but just knowing that feels like enough right now. I don't feel like I'd be missing anything if I turned the job down, especially considering these past few weeks have shown me how great it can be to work for myself. I'm really keen to explore that further.

But I do feel like I'd be missing a lot if I gave up on this second chance with Slater.

I let myself in when I get to his place, just like I have every other time I've been here over the past couple weeks. I know we don't actually have plans to meet right now, but I figure that shouldn't matter...unless that tiny niggling voice in the back of my head is right and he really doesn't want me to stay...

As I move through the hallway I can hear voices in the kitchen. It's Slater and Chance, which I guess shouldn't be too surprising given they both live here. I'm about to interrupt them when I realize the tone of the exchange seems kind of serious.

"So, it's still possible?" I hear Slater saying.

"Technically, yeah," Chance replies. "But I definitely don't recommend it. Both you and Web have already invested so much in this—time, cash...there's so much on the line. Is it really worth it?"

"It is," Slater replies, his voice adamant. "He is."

There's a tense beat of silence before Chance finally replies, "Slate, you know I love Zack, but Web's your family. You guys are like brothers. Do you really want to screw him over for a guy?"

"No, of course I don't. But this isn't just *some guy*," Slater insists. "It's Zack. I can't let him get away again. I need to follow him this time. And it doesn't take a genius to know I can't run this business from Chicago."

I'm rooted to the spot, my eyes wide with alarm as the implications of what I'm hearing register in my mind. On the one hand, I'm feeling all warm and fuzzy from hearing how badly Slater wants to be with me. But on the other, I'm appalled at the thought that my idiotic paranoia could have cost Slater his business. Not to mention his relationship with Web.

Having heard enough, I emerge from behind the corner. "You won't be in Chicago," I say firmly.

Both men startle at the sound of my voice. Slater gazes at me with wide, apprehensive eyes, while Chance clears his throat awkwardly and glances away.

Pushing away from the kitchen counter where they'd been having their conversation, Slater approaches me. "You don't want me to come with you?" he asks, hurt evident in his expression.

I offer an arched brow. "Did you honestly think I'd be okay with you giving up your business, and screwing over Web? Not to mention leaving your house unfinished and moving far away from your family…"

"But—"

I reach out and grab his hand, threading my fingers through his. Offering a soft smile, I tell him, "We're not going anywhere. Neither of us are."

He looks at me in mild confusion. "But the job…"

I shake my head. "I'm not taking the job. And I don't need any more time to figure out whether I want to stay here. I already know the answer to that."

"And just so we're completely on the same page...the answer is yes?"

I let out a soft chuckle. "Yes, dummy. The answer is yes."

Slater's lips stretch into a broad grin that lights his whole face. Then he wraps his arms around my waist and tugs me closer, crashing his mouth down against mine.

"Okay, this is sweet and all, but could you two maybe wait until *after* I've left to start tearing each other's clothes off?" I hear Chance ask in an exasperated voice.

"You have ten seconds," Slater growls before returning his lips to mine.

He backs me against the wall, caging me in with his large frame. As soon as we hear the front door close behind Chance, we're at each other, ripping away layers of clothing and pausing only once we're down to our briefs.

"Can I tell you a secret?" Slater asks as his lips trail over my neck.

I let out a soft hum as his hands slide down my waist to settle on my ass. "Uh huh. I love secrets."

He draws his head back so he can lock gazes with me, those gorgeous chocolate-colored eyes full of raw affection, and maybe a little apprehension. "I never stopped loving you," he admits.

I offer a soft smile and tilt my head up to brush my lips to his. "Same. I tried really, really hard but I couldn't do it."

His face splits into a wide grin. "Same."

His mouth finds mine again, his hands moving up to my waist and tugging me closer so our bodies are flush together, our cocks moving against each other in a desperate search for friction.

Finally tearing his mouth from mine, Slater spins me around to face the wall. Taking my hands in his, he lifts them to brace against the wall, before sliding his palms down my arms and over my back. I let out a shaky breath as his lips touch my shoulders, his breath hot on my skin as he kisses his way down my back, making me shiver in anticipation. Once he's on his knees behind me, his fingers curl around the waistband of my briefs, tugging them down and letting my raging hard cock spring free.

"Jesus, Slater…"

All it takes is one swipe of his tongue over my crease for my legs to start trembling. He lets out a chuckle in response and I feel the vibration of it all around my ass, prompting me to let out a moan of pleasure.

With his large hands bracing my ass in a firm grip, he goes to town swirling his tongue around the sensitive nerves at my entrance. And then he pushes inside and I just about lose it. If I weren't basically sandwiched between Slater and the wall right now, there's no way I'd still be on my feet.

"Slate. Jesus. Fuck. *Ah, I need to come!*"

Much to my dismay, that prompts him to stop what he's doing and get to his feet. I let out a little whimper at the loss of his mouth, but it dies the moment I feel the head of his cock pressing against my hole.

"Not like that," he murmurs in my ear, before piercing my entrance.

He's going so agonizingly slowly I can't help myself from pushing back against him and taking more of his cock inside me.

"Jesus. Fuck, Zack..." Slater pants out, and I can feel his hot, heavy breath on my neck.

"Come on, baby, I need you to fuck me," I say desperately, pushing my ass back again.

"Jesus," he mutters, wrapping his arms tight around me and finally giving me what I want by burying himself the rest of the way in one hard thrust.

"Fuck, yes." The words are mingled with a low moan of pleasure. Jesus, he feels so fucking perfect. He always does.

Slater lets go of my waist, lifting his hands to join mine against the wall, threading our fingers together in a gesture that somehow makes me feel even more connected than we already were. He buries his head in my neck as he snaps his hips, thrusting inside me and hitting me exactly where I need it.

It's not long before I feel the climax building up in me and I'm ready to explode. But before, I can let loose all over the hallway wall, Slater pulls out of me and spins me around. A moment later, I'm in his arms, my legs wrapped around his waist as he thrusts inside me again.

He slams me into the wall, his lips finding mine in a greedy, desperate kiss that I feel in every cell of my body. My hands fly into his hair, tugging at the strands and pulling him even closer.

We groan into each other's mouths, swallowing the sounds with our messy kisses as he continues to thrust inside me, winding me tighter and tighter until, finally...

"Ah, fuck..." I tear my mouth from Slater's, burying my teeth in the side of his neck as my climax rushes through me. It's barely a second later that I feel his hot cum filling me, his grip on my ass like iron as he hurtles over the edge.

I don't know how long we stay like that, with me braced against the wall, my arms and legs wrapped around Slater's beautiful body as we exchange soft, slow kisses, but eventually Slater sets me back on my feet, his arm coming up to wrap around me the second he senses me wobbling on my still-shaky legs.

"You know, you kind of ruined my plan," he says, staring at me with unabashed affection.

I glance at him, a little puzzled. "What plan?"

An adorable blush touches his cheeks as he admits, "I wanted to watch your face when you came."

I let out a soft chuckle. "I guess you'll just have to wait until next time. Or the time after that. Or the time after that." I offer a wide grin and lift my arms to link around his neck again. "Trust me, babe. There's going to be many, many, many, *many* opportunities…"

He smiles hopefully. "You're really staying?"

I nod, and reach up so I can brush a soft kiss over his lips. "I'm really staying."

EPILOGUE

Zack

"Okay, you can't look."

"I'm not looking," I insist.

"You can't even peek."

I let out an aggravated grunt. "Slater, for fuck's sake, I swear I'm not looking." Despite how tempted I am to defy him—and can you blame me with how secretive he's been acting lately? —it's not a feasible option considering his hand is currently slapped so firmly over my eyes it's cutting off circulation to my eyeballs.

Seemingly satisfied, Slater grabs my shoulder with his free hand and starts steering me forward. "Okay, just walk normally and I'll let you know when we get to some steps."

"You could just carry me—that'd be more gallant."

"Then you'd be able to peek," he says, clearly worried.

"I promised you I wouldn't," I say in my most innocent voice. "Don't you trust me?"

He thinks it over for a long moment before finally letting out a heavy sigh. "Fine. But I swear, if you peek you are *so* getting punished later."

I let out a soft chuckle. "That's not exactly an incentive, babe."

"I could punish you by withdrawing sex," Slater suggests,

"Ha! I'd like to see you last a day."

With a grumble of annoyance, he finally moves his hand from my eyes before slipping his arm under my legs and scooping me into his arms.

I can't help it; I open my eyes the tiniest fraction, just to give myself a clue…and find myself looking right into Slater's beautiful and completely unsurprised gaze. He gives a rueful shake of his head but says nothing, so I take that as my cue that I'm allowed to continue peeking.

I can't see much at the angle he's holding me at, but I'm able to tell we're at Slater's house—or 'our house' as he insists on calling it—which isn't exactly surprising considering I knew we were driving out this way.

He's put a ton of work into the house over the past few months and it's at the stage now where it's close to being completely done. All it needs is the final touches, like the lighting, the bathroom fixtures, and the kitchen appliances—all stuff Slater's not able to do himself, which of course frustrates the hell out of him.

He opens the door and carries me through. From way down the hall, I can hear the soft chattering of voices and then a bunch of people whispering things like, "Shh" and, "Be quiet, they're coming!"

Epilogue

"There are people here?" I ask curiously, twisting my head about to strain my ears for more chatter.

"Yeah," Slater grumbles. "And they were *supposed* to stay quiet."

"Slater, you're supposed to wait until the actual wedding night to carry him over the threshold!" someone who sounds a lot like Slater's mom, Genevieve, calls out with a chuckle, clearly ignoring the instructions he'd given her.

"Oh, he's just being romantic," a voice that most definitely belongs to Nora says.

"I don't know about that," George says. "Maybe Zack just hurt his ankle or something. He looks like he's in pain."

My whole body starts shaking with laughter, prompting Slater to curse under his breath.

"That'd be an awfully big coincidence, don't you think?" Harriett, I think, says to her brother.

I'm not sure whether it's because he's given up on his plan going smoothly, or because it was supposed to happen at this point anyway, but Slater sets me down in front of him and tells me to open my eyes.

When I do, I see a whole bunch of Goodes, as well as my mother, crowded in front of me, all standing under a big, glittery banner that reads *CONGRATULATIONS!*

At first, I think this celebration must have something to do with the house, because, looking around, I can see that all the work that needed to be done is finished and the place now looks a hundred percent livable.

But then I turn behind me to find Slater down on one

knee, a ring box in hand. My hand flies to my mouth, my eyes wide with surprise.

This is *so* not what I was expecting. We've only been back together for four months. But at the same time, I can't deny that I've been happier in the past few months than I ever imagined possible, and despite that nagging logical part of my brain telling me it's too soon, I know deep down this is right. So, for once in my life, I let my heart make the decision for me.

A wide smile spreads across my face as I nod. "If that's what I think it is, the answer's yes."

Slater's whole face lights up with his smile and he surges to his feet, wrapping his arms around me and lifting me from the ground. Everyone behind us starts cheering and clapping, which startles me for a second because I'd completely forgotten they were there.

Slater sets me back down and opens the ring box, revealing a simple platinum ring with a beautiful woven pattern; it's perfect. He removes the ring from the box and places it at the end of my finger. Lifting his glance to meet my eyes, he murmurs, "Will you marry me, Zack?"

I smile affectionately at him. "I already told you, the answer's yes. It'll always be yes, no matter what you ask me."

He smirks at me, one eyebrow arched. "Even if I kill someone and ask for help burying the body?"

"Even then," I assure him, reaching up to wrap my hands around his neck and draw him toward me for soft, sweet kiss, which draws applause from the crowd behind us that I'd once again forgotten about.

Epilogue

SLATER

I'm not sure whose idea it was to do the bachelor party in Vegas. It just kind of happened one night when Lawson was over and he and Zack were watching their favorite show—*Real Vegas Weddings.* Lawson joked that we should get married in Vegas, which was a suggestion that of course got shot down pretty quickly. But then the bachelor party idea came up and we ended up just rolling with it.

So now we're here in Vegas with all our closest friends, enjoying our last weekend before we tie the knot next week. It's been fun, but honestly I'm kind of ready to ditch the bar crawl and take Zack back to our fancy suite right now. I don't quite get that whole needing one last night of freedom thing; it's not like getting married is a prison sentence. Well, at least it doesn't feel that way to me.

"Hey, babe, have you seen Jesse?" Zack asks as he sidles up to me while I wait to be served at the bar of the new club we've just arrived at. I think this makes it number five for the night. Ask George and Lawson—they're the ones in charge of the itinerary.

I frown at him. "No, I haven't. It's weird, I was just thinking I haven't seen Web for a while either."

Zack's brows shoot up. "What do you think the odds are that one of them has killed the other and is now on their way out to the desert to bury the body?"

I offer him a considering look. "I'd say pretty high."

"Do you think we should look into getting new best men?"

I wave a dismissive hand. "If they don't show up by next week we'll look into promoting Law and Axel."

Zack nods, his lips curving up in a wry smile. "Good plan."

Deciding to forgo the drink I'd been about to order, I take Zack's hand and lead him away from the bar. I draw him close to me, tilting my head down to brush a kiss against the side of his mouth. "Can you believe it's only a week away?"

He grins, eyes twinkling with levity as he asks, "You sure you don't want to just ditch next week and get married while we're here?"

I arch a skeptical brow. "And face Nanna's wrath?"

He chuckles. "Good point."

"What I *would* like to do while we're here is make use of our awesome suite…"

Zack's eyes light in anticipation; he squeezes my hand firmly as he starts tugging me toward the club's exit. "Let's go."

❄

ALSO BY ISLA OLSEN

Love & Luck

Fake it 'til You Make Out (Declan's Book)
Virtually Screwed (Owen's Book)
Crazy Little Fling (Shay's Book)
Hopeless Bromantics (Brendan's Book)
Two Men and a Baby (Connor's Book)
Can't Get You Out of My Bed (Aidan's Book)
O Come, All Ye Kellys (Christmas Collection)
Sex, Tries, and Videotape (Finn's Book) - coming 2021

Royal & Reckless

The King and Jai (Lukas's Book)
Three's a Crown (Aleksandr's Book) - coming 2021

Suits & Sevens

Mr. Big Shot (Spencer's Book)
Mr. Right Now (Sullivan's Book) - coming 2021

The Goode Life

Clean Slate (Slater's Book)
Web of Lies (Web's Book) - coming 2021

Lakeview Resort Holiday Stories

The Ghosts of Crushes Past (Evan & Tyler)

Ex-Mas Present (Adrian & Dante)